Radio Delby

Facebook: **facebook.com/idwpublishing**
Twitter: **@idwpublishing**
YouTube: **youtube.com/idwpublishing**
Tumblr: **tumblr.idwpublishing.com**
Instagram: **instagram.com/idwpublishing**

ISBN: 978-1-68405-448-0   22 21 20 19   1 2 3 4

TRANSLATION BY
ANNA ROSENWONG

LETTERING BY
FRANK CVETKOVIC

COLLECTION EDITS BY
JUSTIN EISINGER AND
ALONZO SIMON

COLLECTION DESIGN BY
RON ESTEVEZ

PUBLISHER:
GREG GOLDSTEIN

Greg Goldstein, President and Publisher
John Barber, Editor-In-Chief
Robbie Robbins, EVP/Sr. Art Director
Cara Morrison, Chief Financial Officer
Matt Ruzicka, Chief Accounting Officer
Anita Frazier, SVP of Sales and Marketing
David Hedgecock, Associate Publisher
Jerry Bennington, VP of New Product Development
Lorelei Bunjes, VP of Digital Services
Justin Eisinger, Editorial Director, Graphic Novels & Collections
Eric Moss, Senior Director, Licensing and Business Development

Ted Adams, IDW Founder

Radio Delley

Written by Álex Martínez
Illustrated by Xavier Bonet

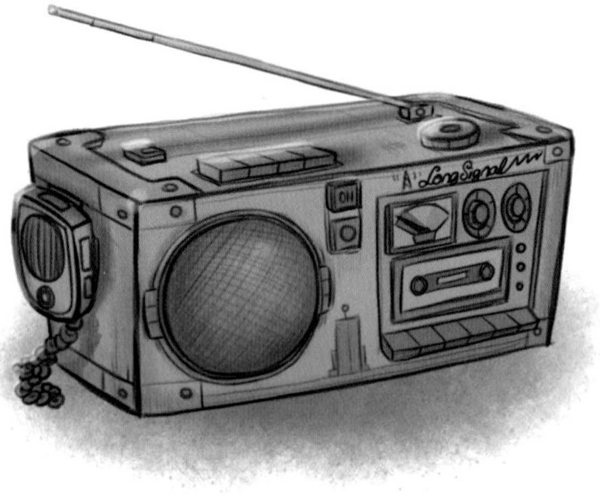
"A" Long Signal
ON

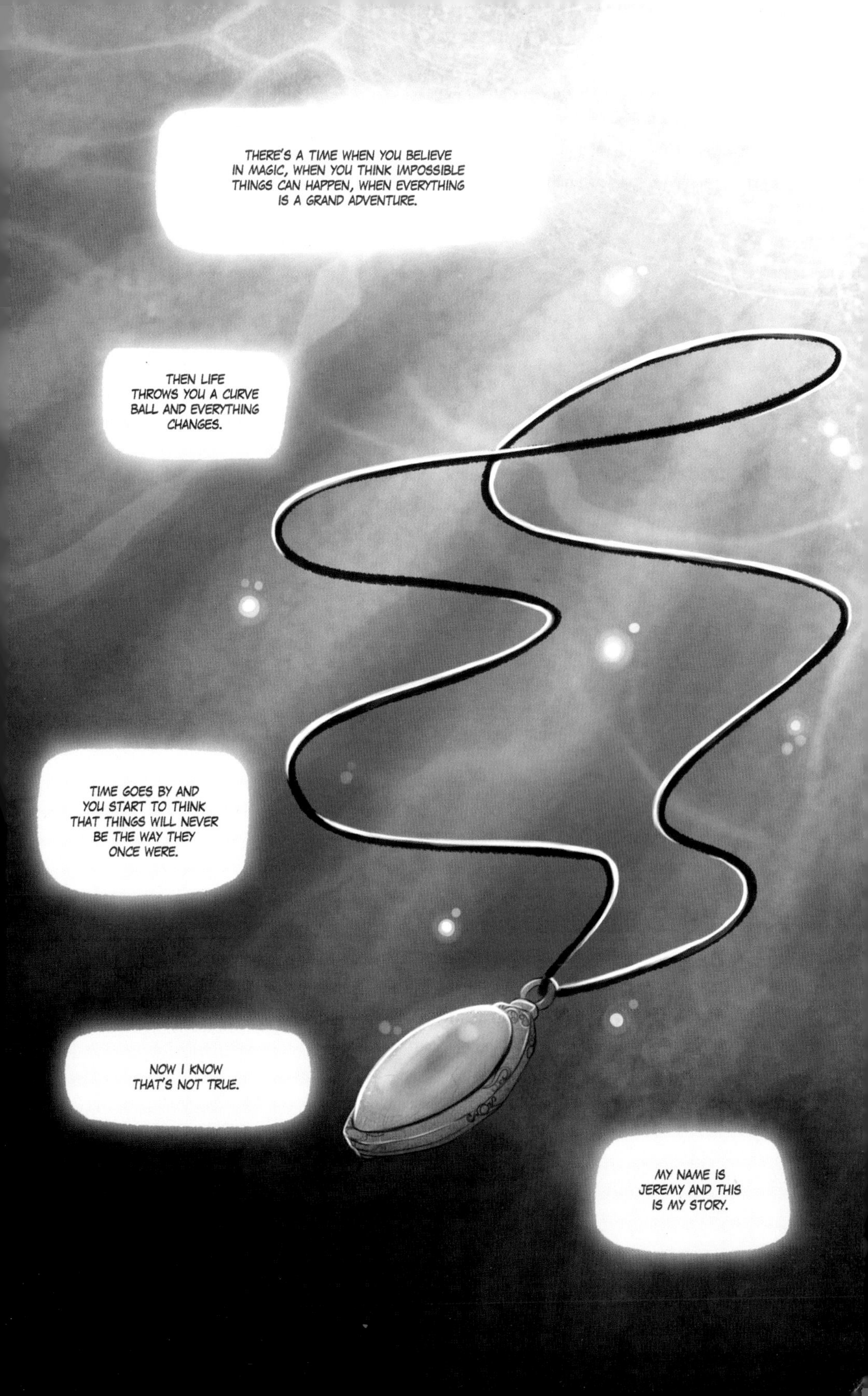
THERE'S A TIME WHEN YOU BELIEVE IN MAGIC, WHEN YOU THINK IMPOSSIBLE THINGS CAN HAPPEN, WHEN EVERYTHING IS A GRAND ADVENTURE.
THEN LIFE THROWS YOU A CURVE BALL AND EVERYTHING CHANGES.
TIME GOES BY AND YOU START TO THINK THAT THINGS WILL NEVER BE THE WAY THEY ONCE WERE.
NOW I KNOW THAT'S NOT TRUE.
MY NAME IS JEREMY AND THIS IS MY STORY.

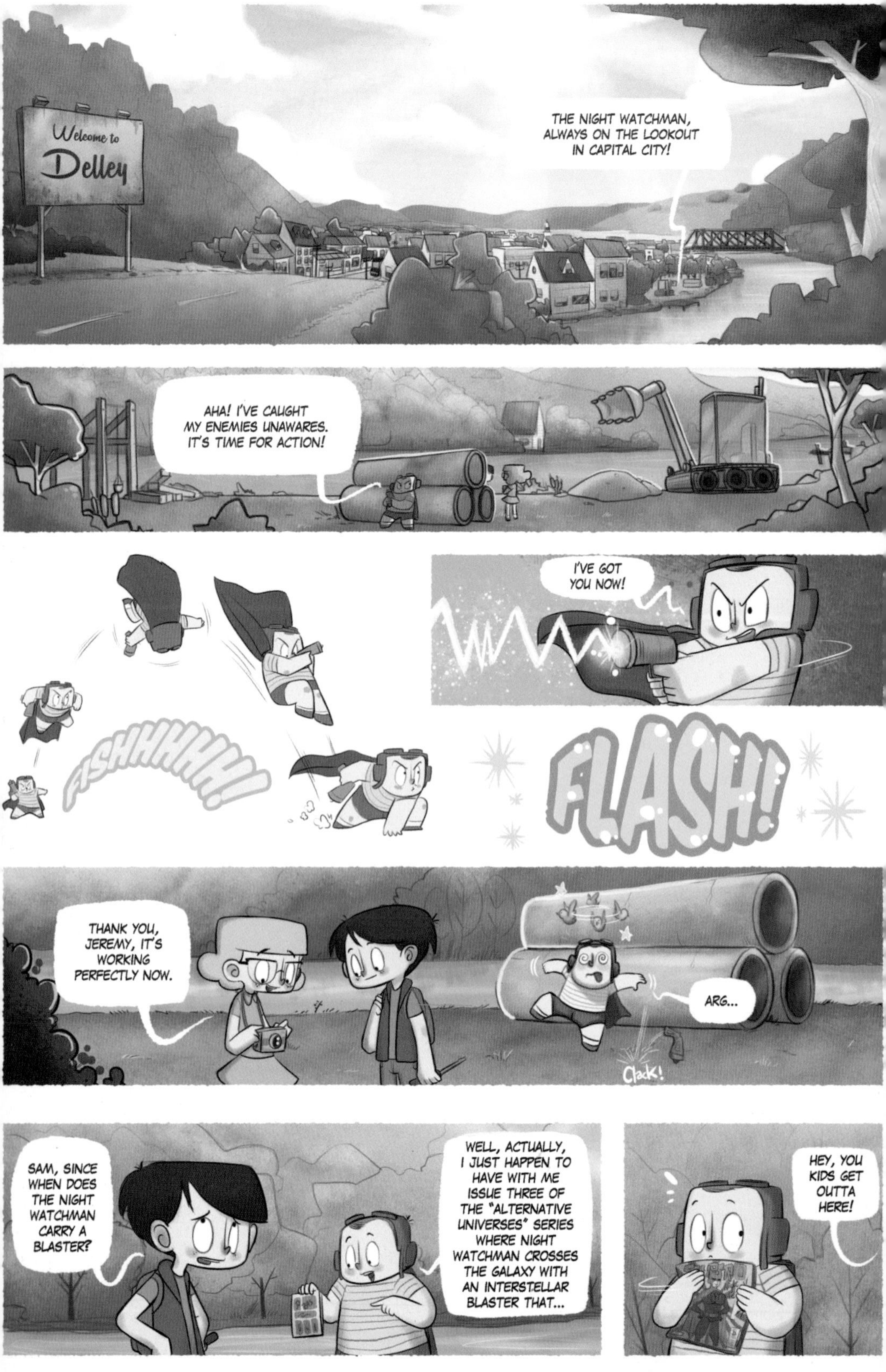
Welcome to Delley
THE NIGHT WATCHMAN, ALWAYS ON THE LOOKOUT IN CAPITAL CITY!
AHA! I'VE CAUGHT MY ENEMIES UNAWARES. IT'S TIME FOR ACTION!
FISHHHHHH!
I'VE GOT YOU NOW!
FLASH!
THANK YOU, JEREMY, IT'S WORKING PERFECTLY NOW.
ARG...
Clack!
SAM, SINCE WHEN DOES THE NIGHT WATCHMAN CARRY A BLASTER?
WELL, ACTUALLY, I JUST HAPPEN TO HAVE WITH ME ISSUE THREE OF THE "ALTERNATIVE UNIVERSES" SERIES WHERE NIGHT WATCHMAN CROSSES THE GALAXY WITH AN INTERSTELLAR BLASTER THAT...
HEY, YOU KIDS GET OUTTA HERE!

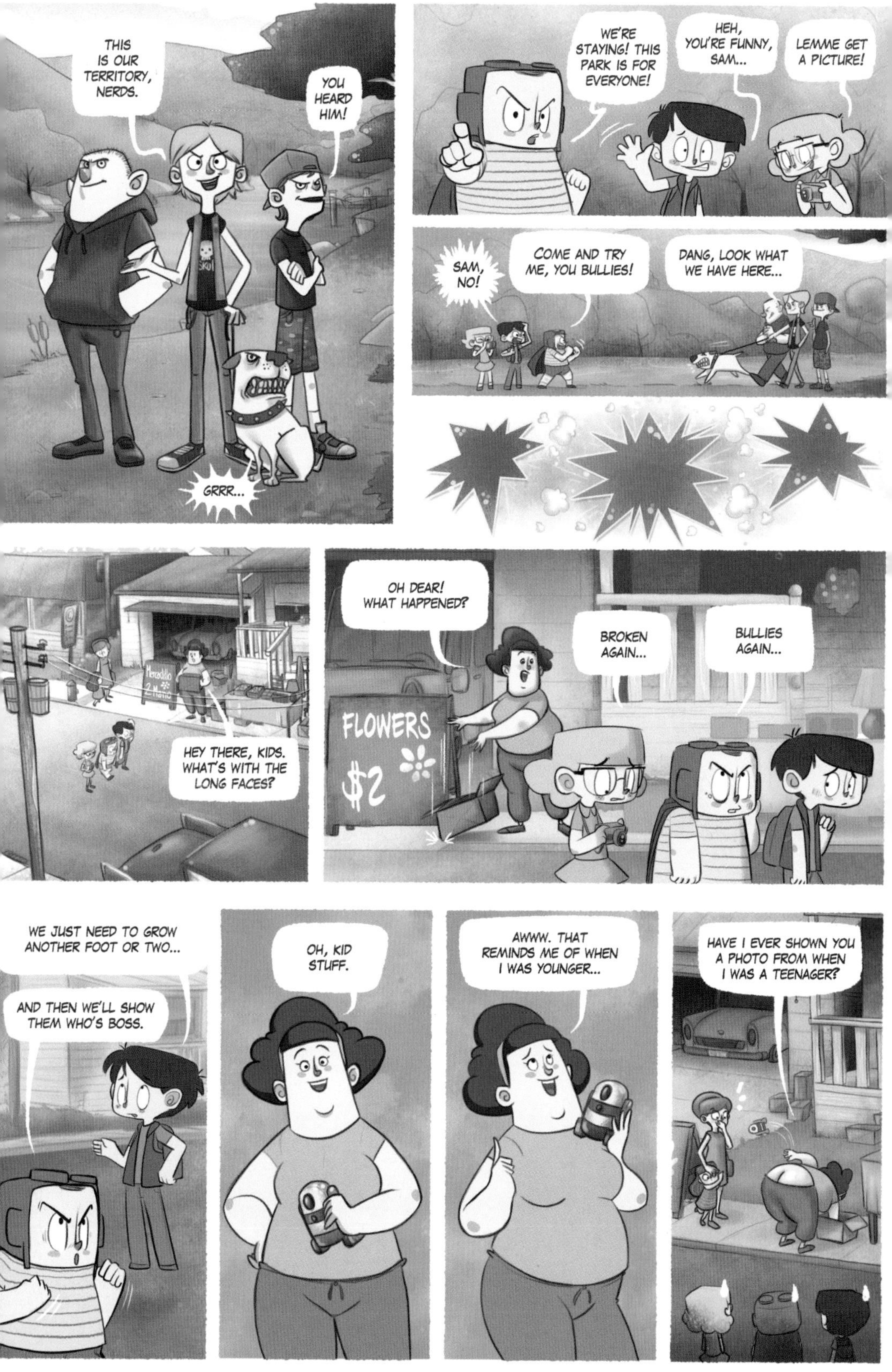
THIS IS OUR TERRITORY, NERDS.
YOU HEARD HIM!
GRRR...
WE'RE STAYING! THIS PARK IS FOR EVERYONE!
HEH, YOU'RE FUNNY, SAM...
LEMME GET A PICTURE!
SAM, NO!
COME AND TRY ME, YOU BULLIES!
DANG, LOOK WHAT WE HAVE HERE...
HEY THERE, KIDS. WHAT'S WITH THE LONG FACES?
OH DEAR! WHAT HAPPENED?
FLOWERS $2
BROKEN AGAIN...
BULLIES AGAIN...
WE JUST NEED TO GROW ANOTHER FOOT OR TWO...
AND THEN WE'LL SHOW THEM WHO'S BOSS.
OH, KID STUFF.
AWWW. THAT REMINDS ME OF WHEN I WAS YOUNGER...
HAVE I EVER SHOWN YOU A PHOTO FROM WHEN I WAS A TEENAGER?

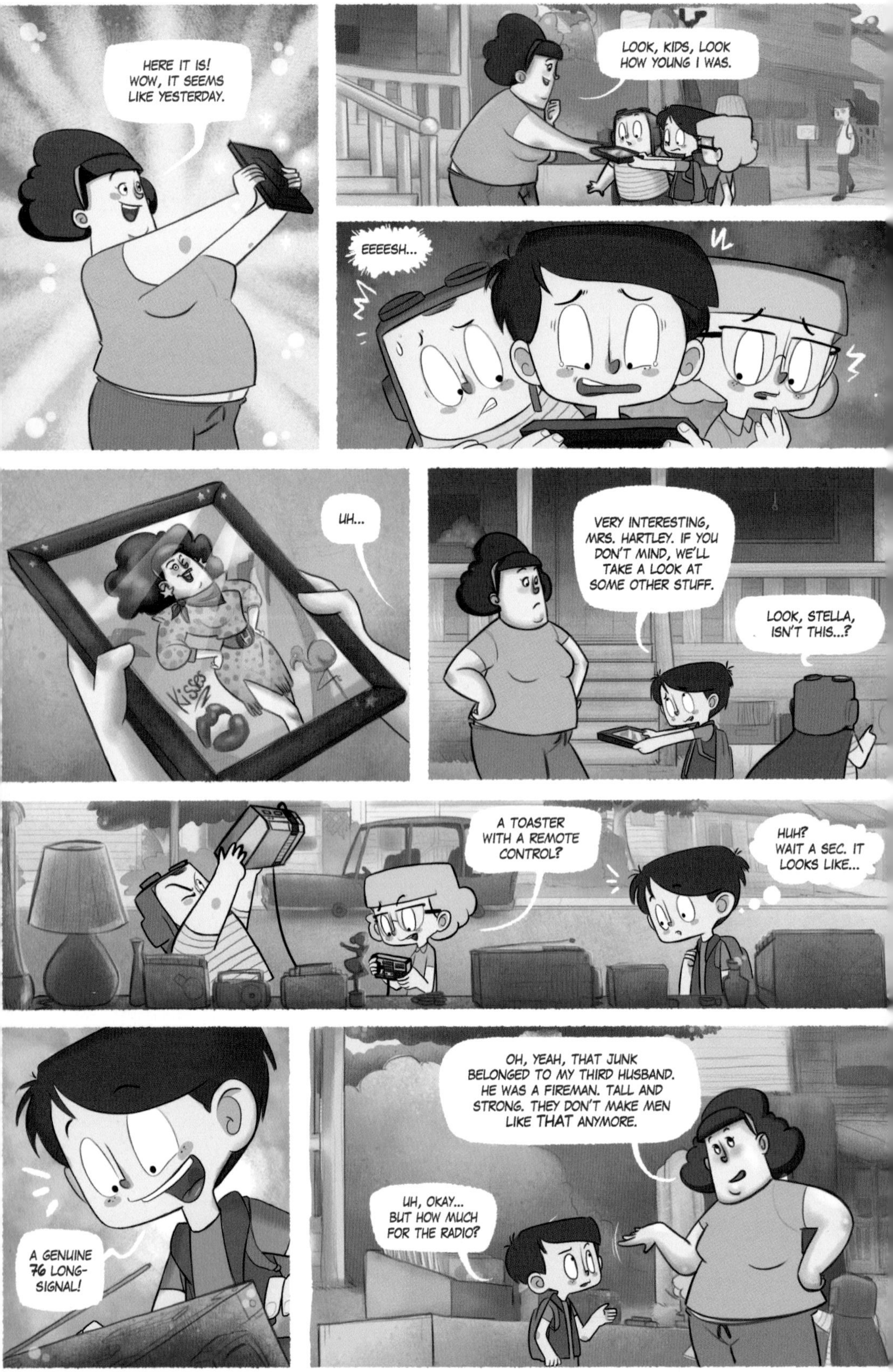
HERE IT IS! WOW, IT SEEMS LIKE YESTERDAY.
LOOK, KIDS, LOOK HOW YOUNG I WAS.
EEEESH...
UH...
KISSES
VERY INTERESTING, MRS. HARTLEY. IF YOU DON'T MIND, WE'LL TAKE A LOOK AT SOME OTHER STUFF.
LOOK, STELLA, ISN'T THIS...?
A TOASTER WITH A REMOTE CONTROL?
HUH? WAIT A SEC. IT LOOKS LIKE...
A GENUINE 76 LONG-SIGNAL!
OH, YEAH, THAT JUNK BELONGED TO MY THIRD HUSBAND. HE WAS A FIREMAN. TALL AND STRONG. THEY DON'T MAKE MEN LIKE THAT ANYMORE.
UH, OKAY... BUT HOW MUCH FOR THE RADIO?

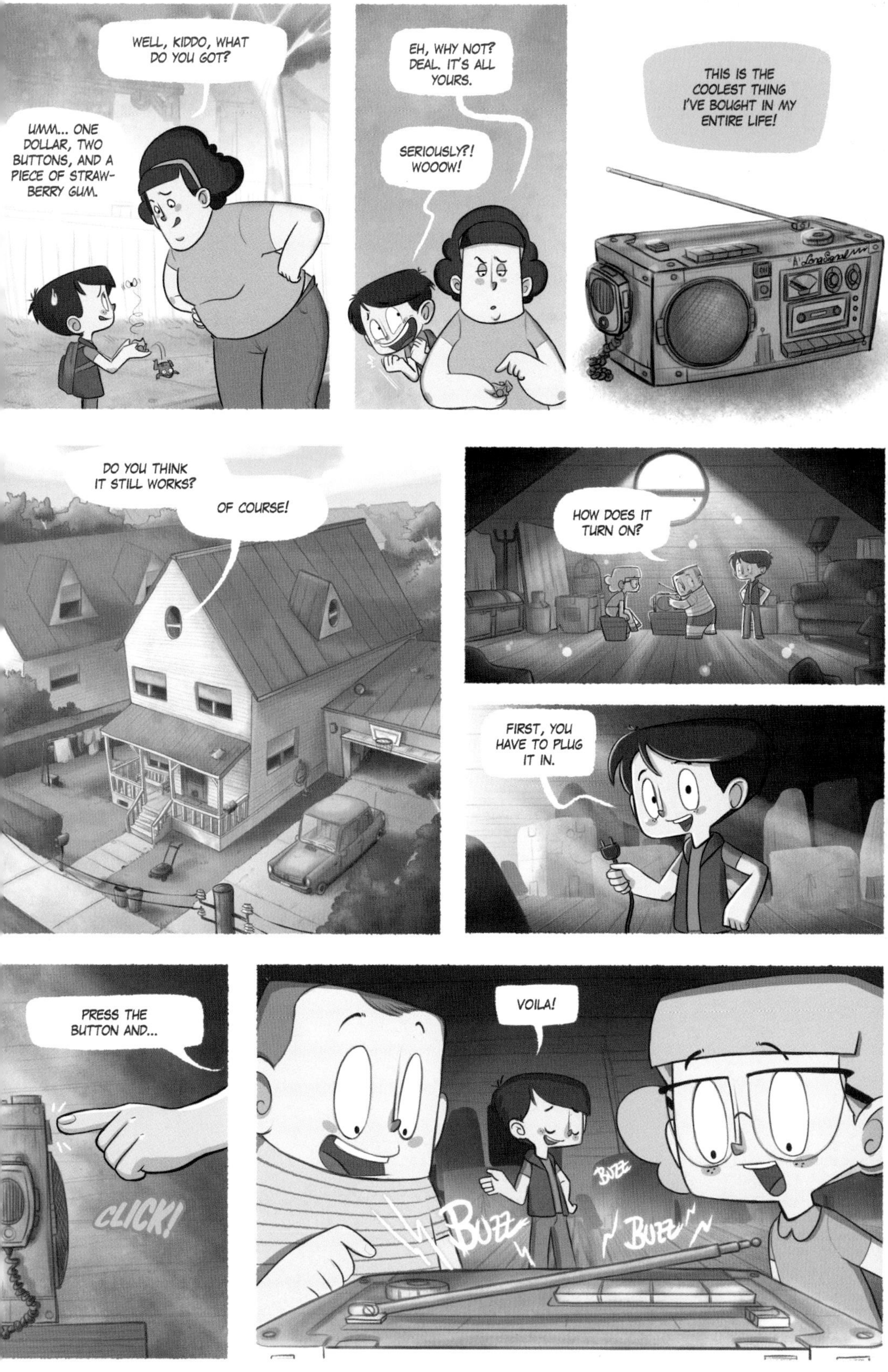
WELL, KIDDO, WHAT DO YOU GOT?
UMM... ONE DOLLAR, TWO BUTTONS, AND A PIECE OF STRAW-BERRY GUM.
EH, WHY NOT? DEAL. IT'S ALL YOURS.
SERIOUSLY?! WOOOW!
THIS IS THE COOLEST THING I'VE BOUGHT IN MY ENTIRE LIFE!
DO YOU THINK IT STILL WORKS?
OF COURSE!
HOW DOES IT TURN ON?
FIRST, YOU HAVE TO PLUG IT IN.
PRESS THE BUTTON AND...
CLICK!
VOILA!
BUZZ
BUZZ
BUZZ

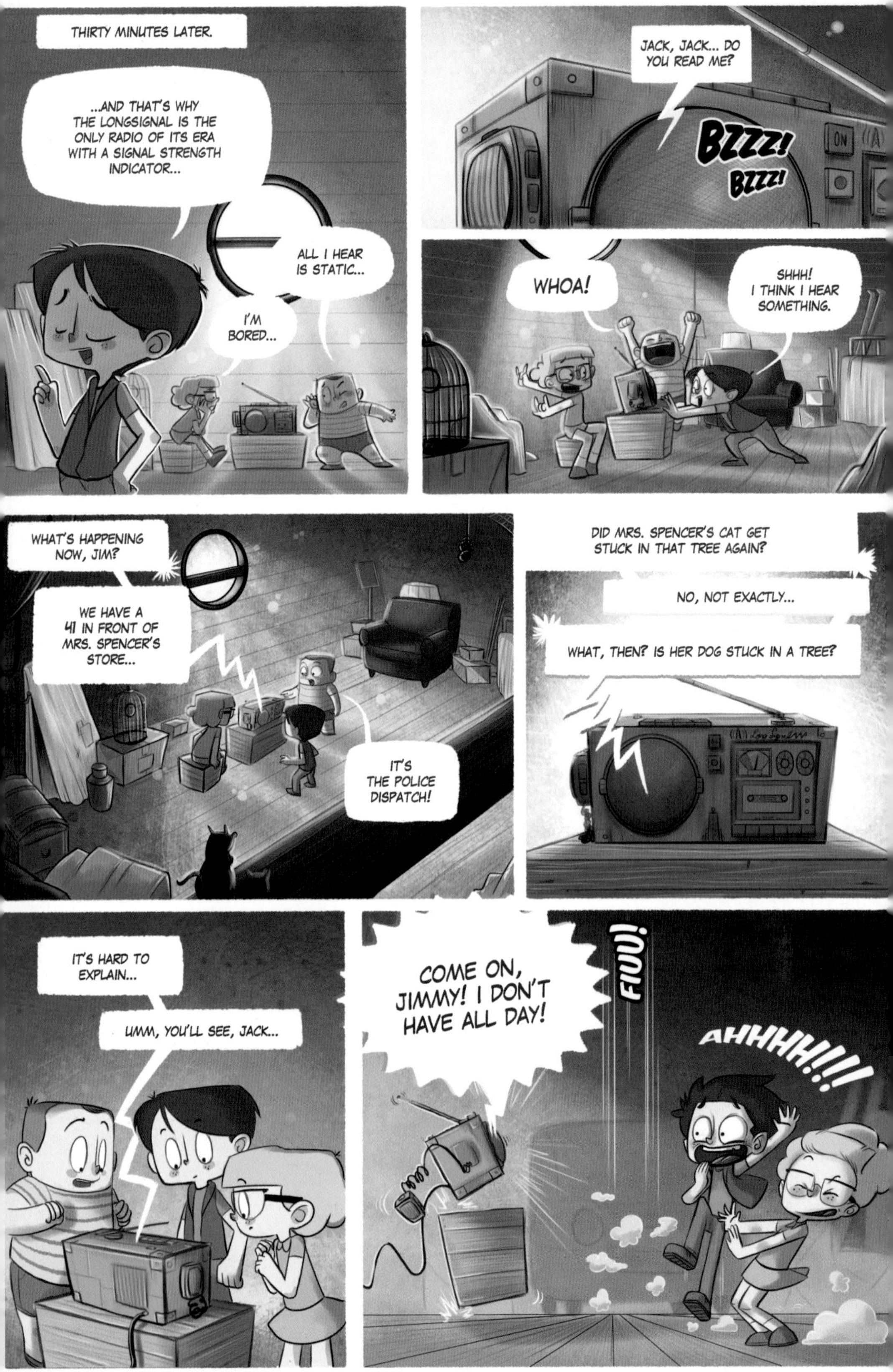
THIRTY MINUTES LATER.
...AND THAT'S WHY THE LONGSIGNAL IS THE ONLY RADIO OF ITS ERA WITH A SIGNAL STRENGTH INDICATOR...
ALL I HEAR IS STATIC...
I'M BORED...
JACK, JACK... DO YOU READ ME?
BZZZ!
BZZZ!
ON
WHOA!
SHHH! I THINK I HEAR SOMETHING.
WHAT'S HAPPENING NOW, JIM?
WE HAVE A 41 IN FRONT OF MRS. SPENCER'S STORE...
IT'S THE POLICE DISPATCH!
DID MRS. SPENCER'S CAT GET STUCK IN THAT TREE AGAIN?
NO, NOT EXACTLY...
WHAT, THEN? IS HER DOG STUCK IN A TREE?
IT'S HARD TO EXPLAIN...
UMM, YOU'LL SEE, JACK...
COME ON, JIMMY! I DON'T HAVE ALL DAY!
FIUU!
AHHHH!!!!

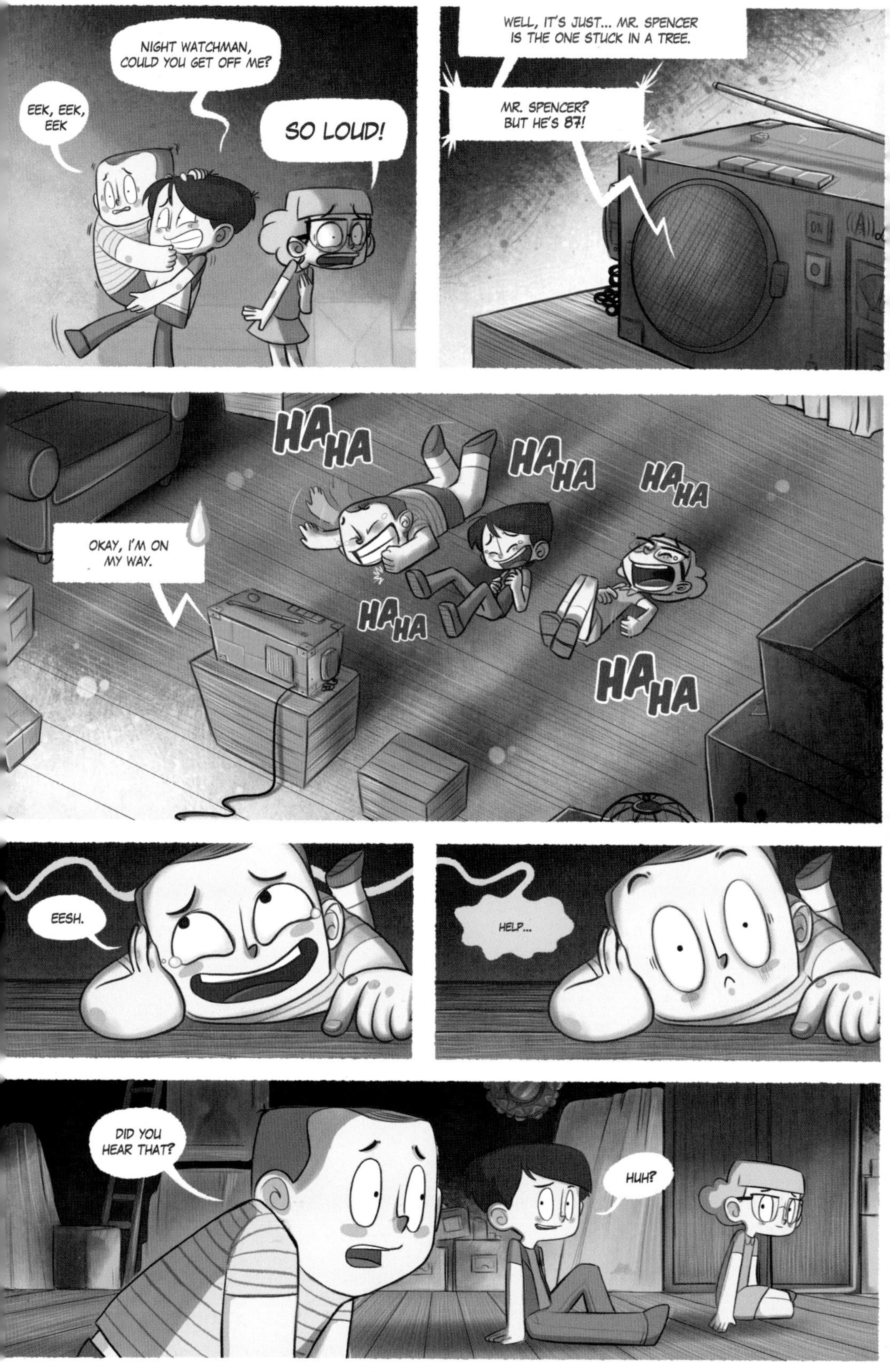
EEK, EEK, EEK
NIGHT WATCHMAN, COULD YOU GET OFF ME?
SO LOUD!
WELL, IT'S JUST... MR. SPENCER IS THE ONE STUCK IN A TREE.
MR. SPENCER? BUT HE'S 87!
HAHA
HAHA
HAHA
OKAY, I'M ON MY WAY.
HAHA
HAHA
EESH.
HELP...
DID YOU HEAR THAT?
HUH?

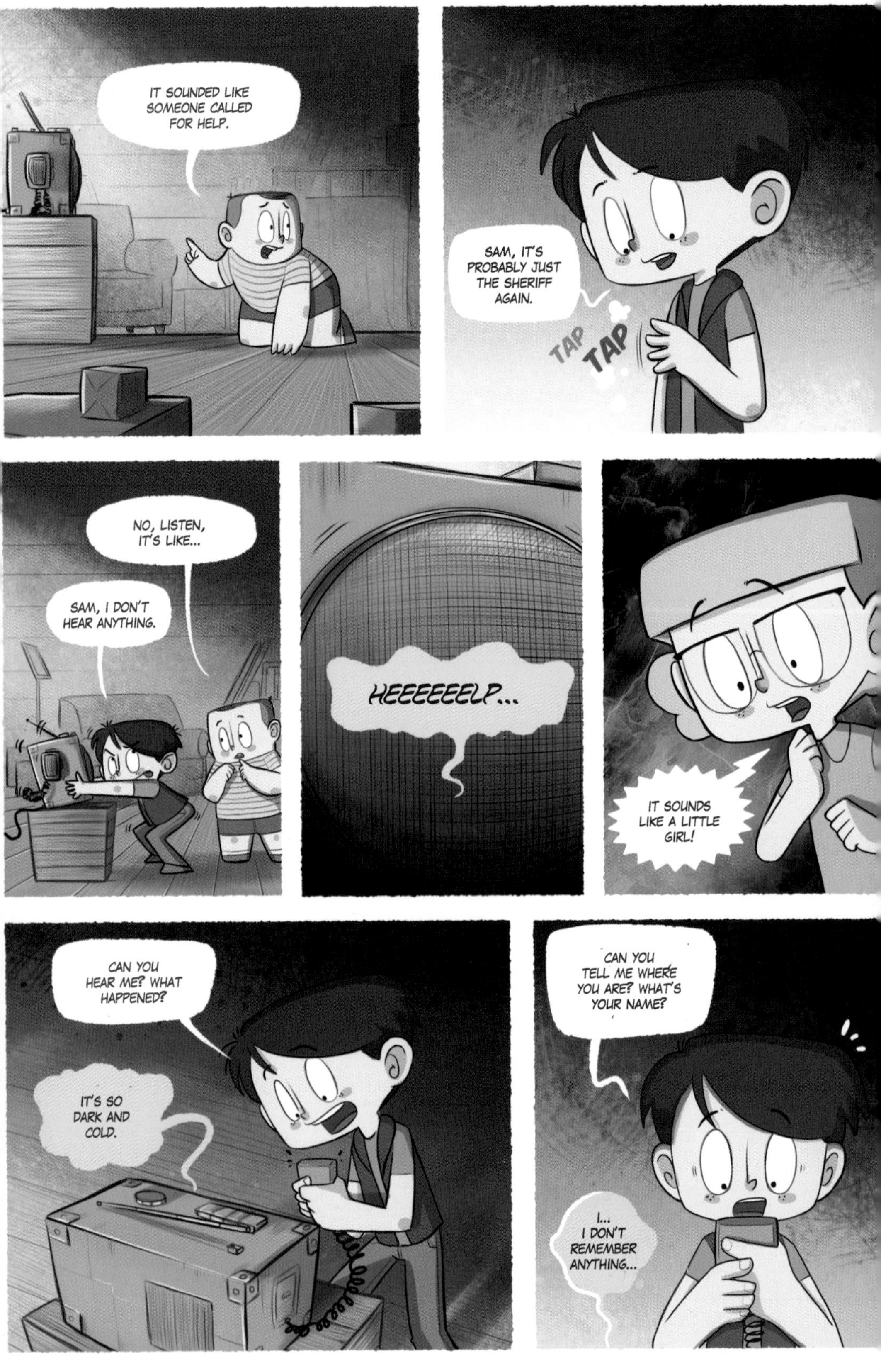
IT SOUNDED LIKE SOMEONE CALLED FOR HELP.
SAM, IT'S PROBABLY JUST THE SHERIFF AGAIN.
TAP TAP
NO, LISTEN, IT'S LIKE...
SAM, I DON'T HEAR ANYTHING.
HEEEEEELP...
IT SOUNDS LIKE A LITTLE GIRL!
CAN YOU HEAR ME? WHAT HAPPENED?
IT'S SO DARK AND COLD.
CAN YOU TELL ME WHERE YOU ARE? WHAT'S YOUR NAME?
I... I DON'T REMEMBER ANYTHING...

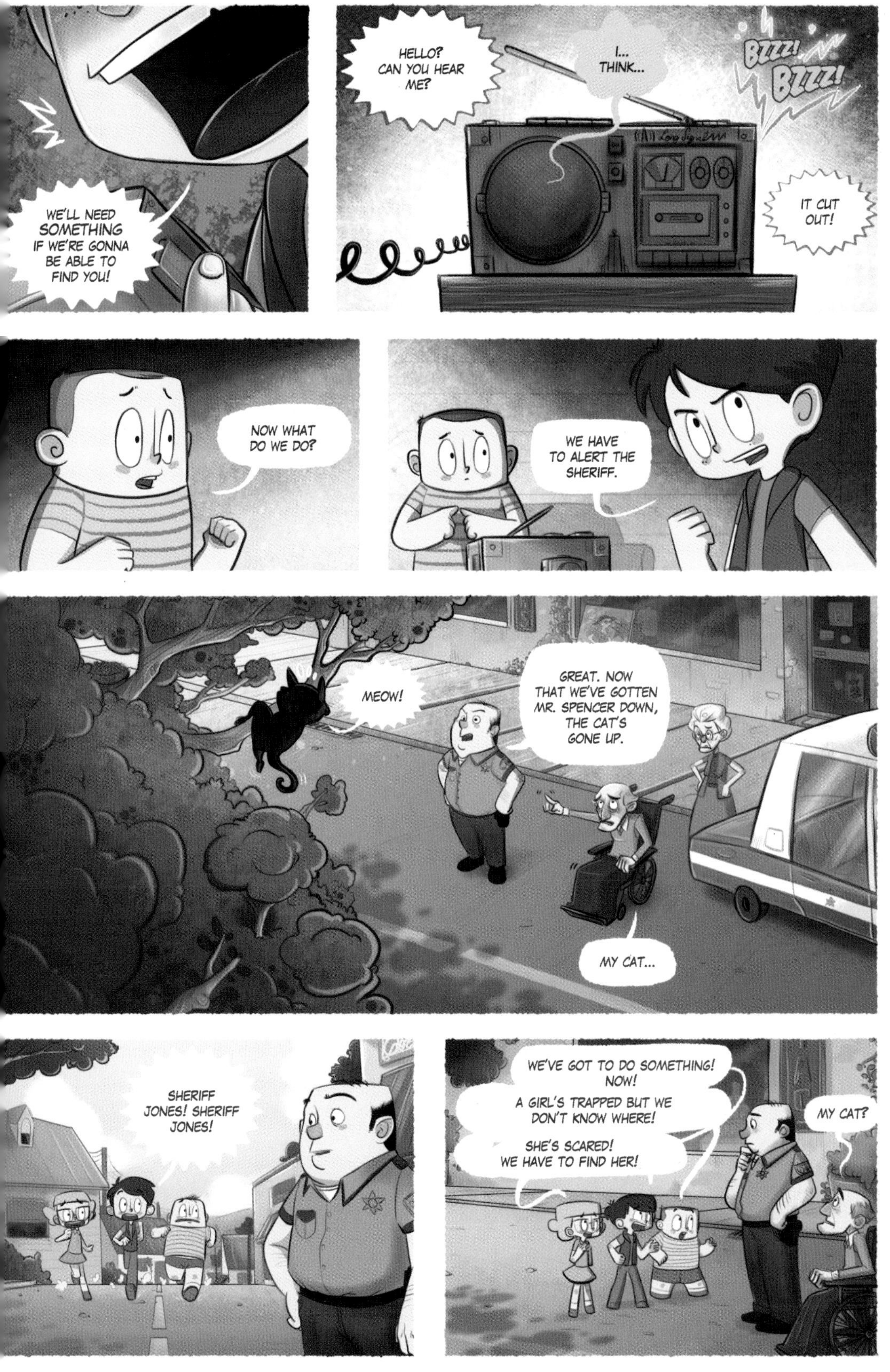
WE'LL NEED SOMETHING IF WE'RE GONNA BE ABLE TO FIND YOU!
HELLO? CAN YOU HEAR ME?
I... THINK...
BZZZ! BZZZ!
IT CUT OUT!
NOW WHAT DO WE DO?
WE HAVE TO ALERT THE SHERIFF.
MEOW!
GREAT. NOW THAT WE'VE GOTTEN MR. SPENCER DOWN, THE CAT'S GONE UP.
MY CAT...
SHERIFF JONES! SHERIFF JONES!
WE'VE GOT TO DO SOMETHING! NOW!
A GIRL'S TRAPPED BUT WE DON'T KNOW WHERE!
SHE'S SCARED! WE HAVE TO FIND HER!
MY CAT?

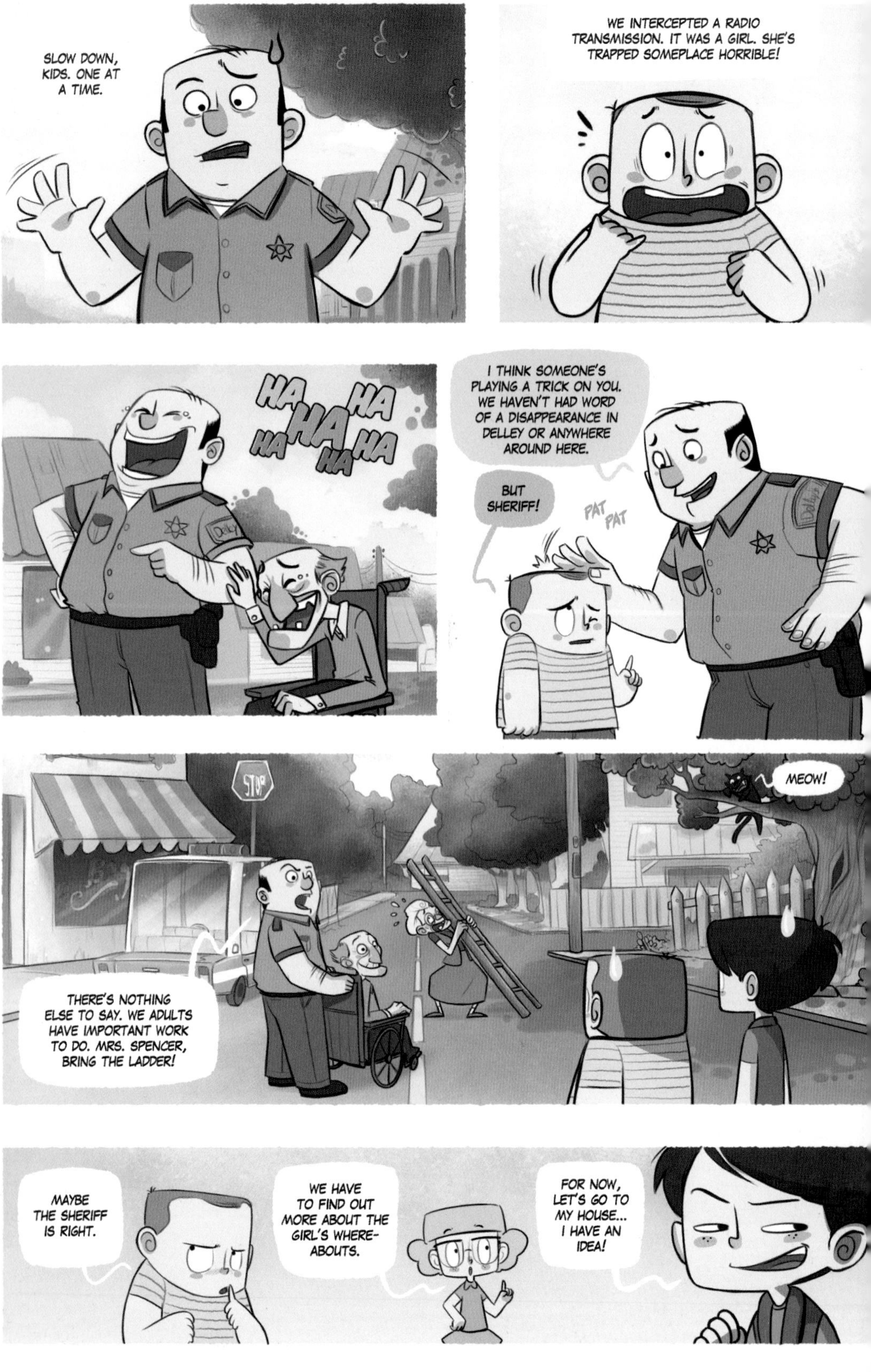
SLOW DOWN, KIDS. ONE AT A TIME.
WE INTERCEPTED A RADIO TRANSMISSION. IT WAS A GIRL. SHE'S TRAPPED SOMEPLACE HORRIBLE!
HA HA HA HA HA HA
I THINK SOMEONE'S PLAYING A TRICK ON YOU. WE HAVEN'T HAD WORD OF A DISAPPEARANCE IN DELLEY OR ANYWHERE AROUND HERE.
BUT SHERIFF!
PAT PAT
STOP
MEOW!
THERE'S NOTHING ELSE TO SAY. WE ADULTS HAVE IMPORTANT WORK TO DO. MRS. SPENCER, BRING THE LADDER!
MAYBE THE SHERIFF IS RIGHT.
WE HAVE TO FIND OUT MORE ABOUT THE GIRL'S WHERE-ABOUTS.
FOR NOW, LET'S GO TO MY HOUSE... I HAVE AN IDEA!

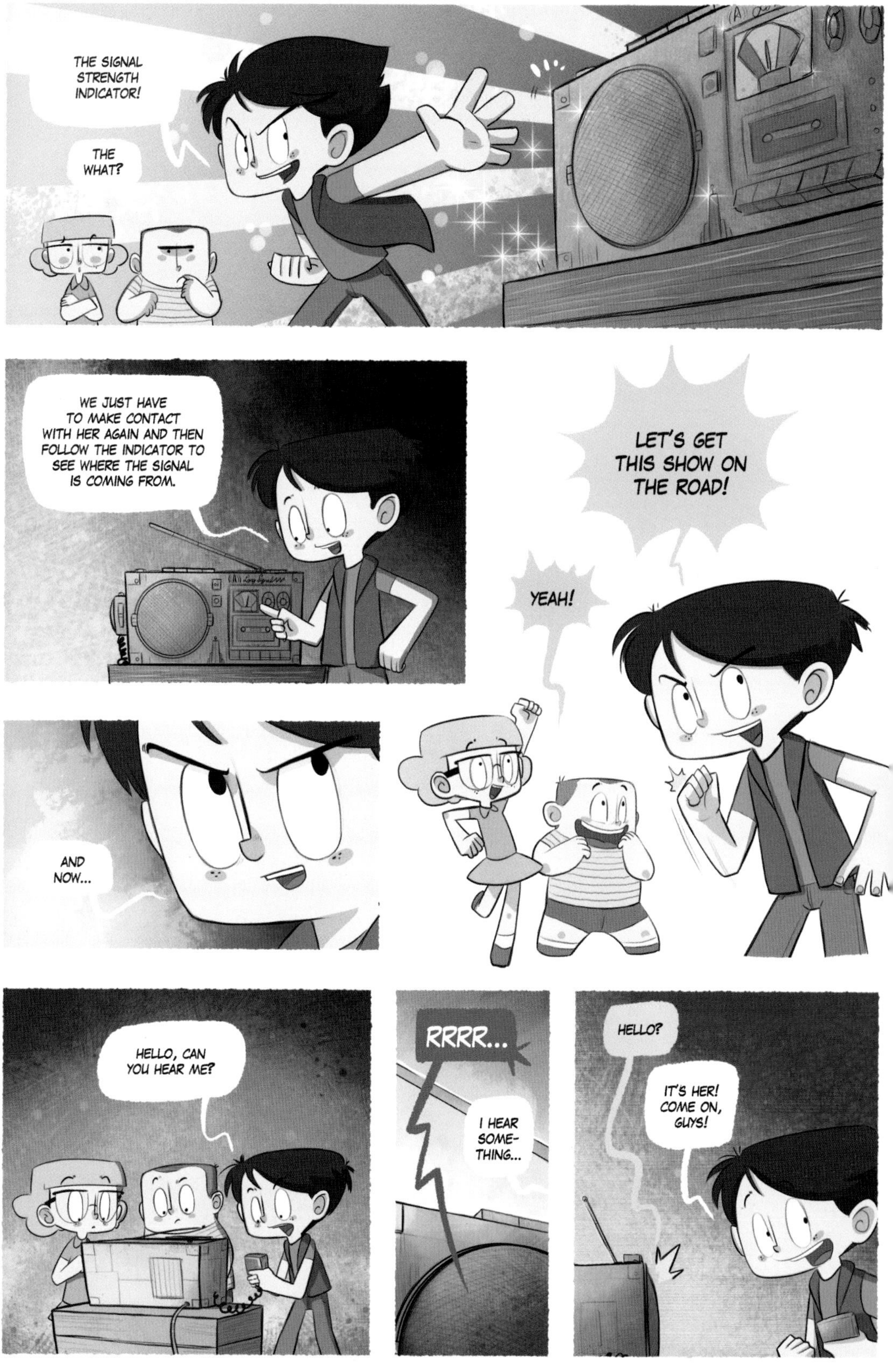

THE SIGNAL STRENGTH INDICATOR!
THE WHAT?
WE JUST HAVE TO MAKE CONTACT WITH HER AGAIN AND THEN FOLLOW THE INDICATOR TO SEE WHERE THE SIGNAL IS COMING FROM.
AND NOW...
LET'S GET THIS SHOW ON THE ROAD!
YEAH!
HELLO, CAN YOU HEAR ME?
RRRR...
I HEAR SOME-THING...
HELLO?
IT'S HER! COME ON, GUYS!

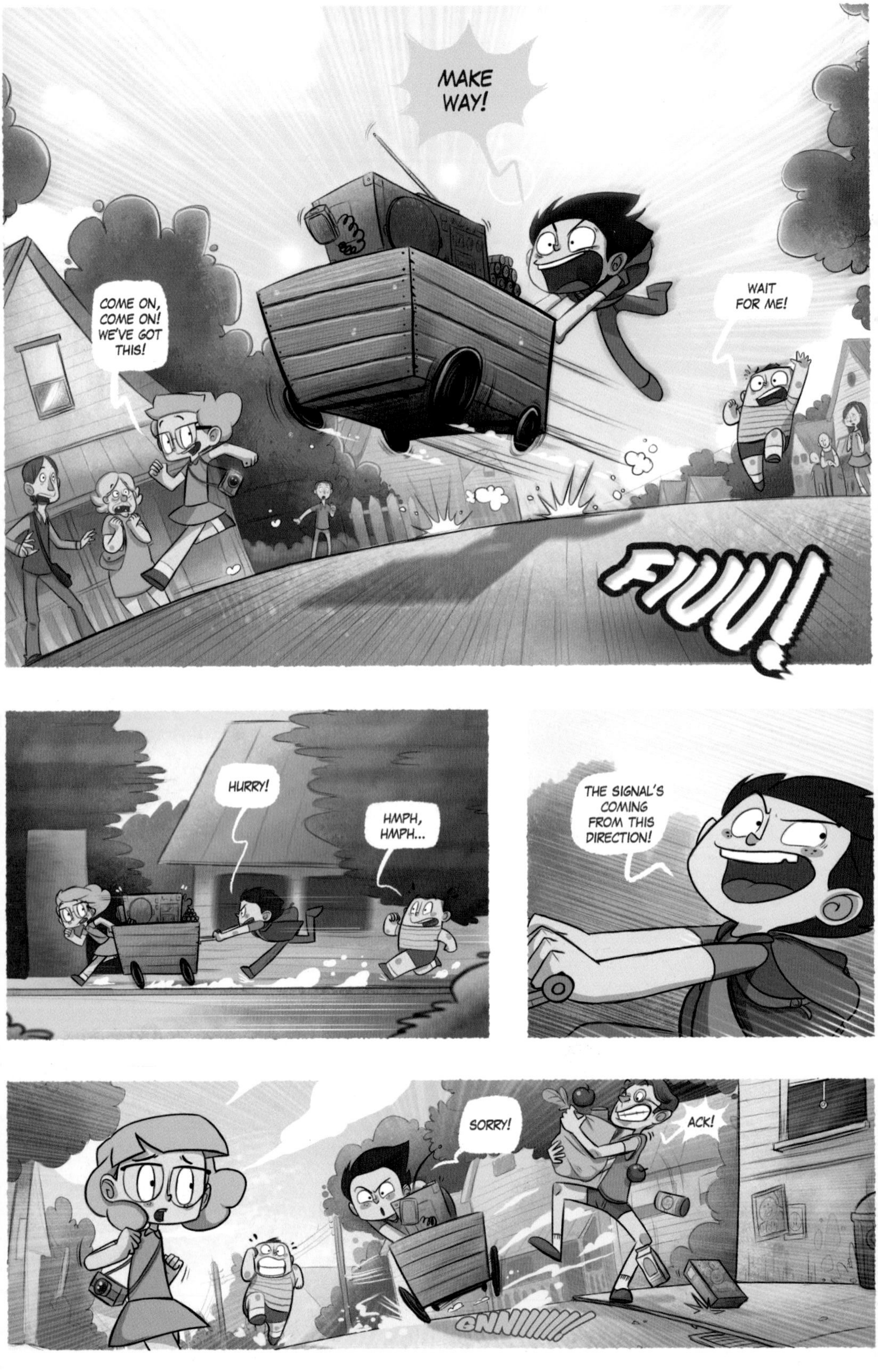
MAKE WAY!
COME ON, COME ON! WE'VE GOT THIS!
WAIT FOR ME!
FIUU!
HURRY!
HMPH, HMPH...
THE SIGNAL'S COMING FROM THIS DIRECTION!
SORRY!
ACK!
GNN!!!!!!!

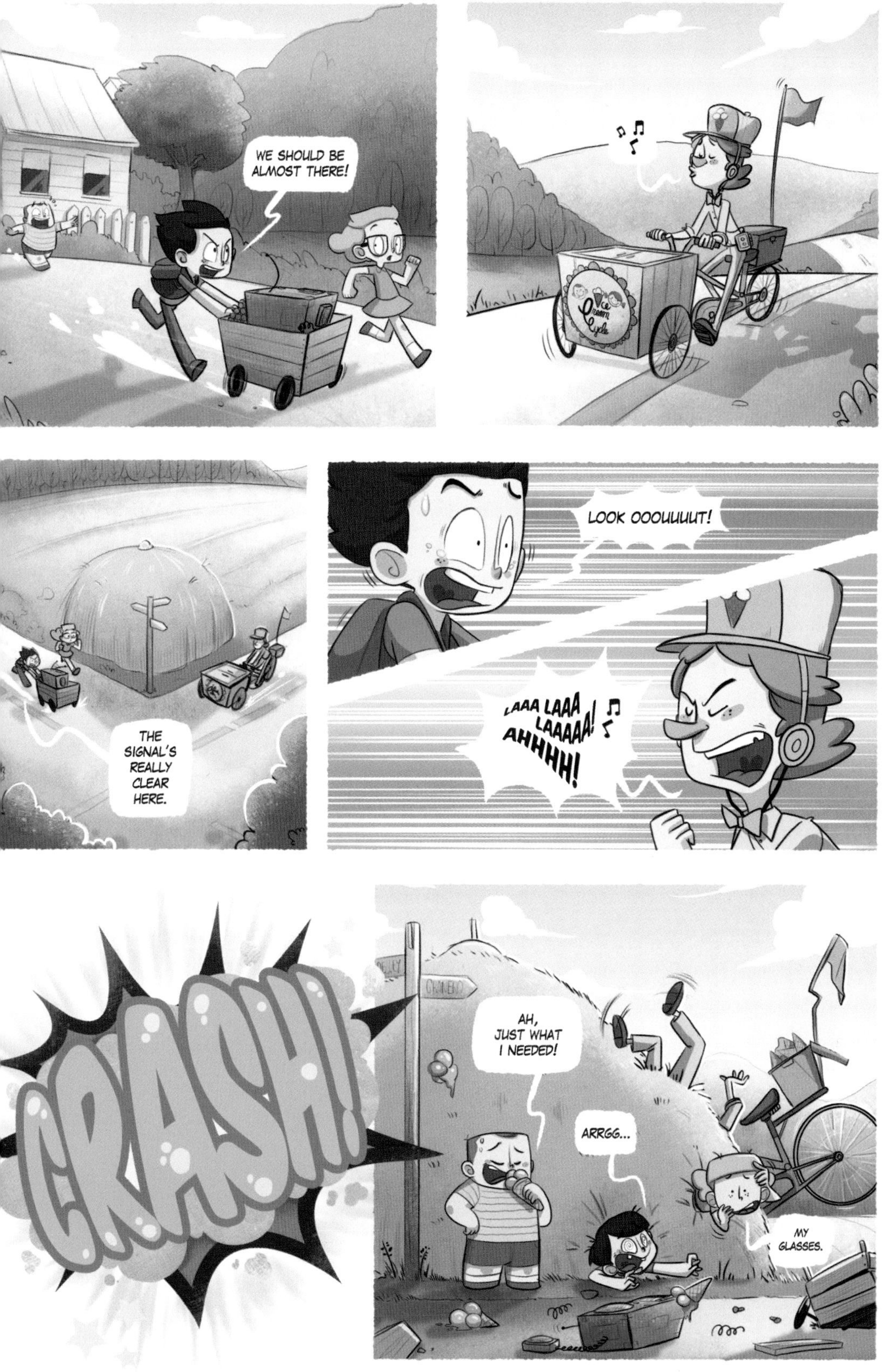
WE SHOULD BE ALMOST THERE!
THE SIGNAL'S REALLY CLEAR HERE.
LOOK OOOUUUUT!
LAAA LAAA LAAAAA! AHHHH!
CRASH!
AH, JUST WHAT I NEEDED!
ARRGG...
MY GLASSES.

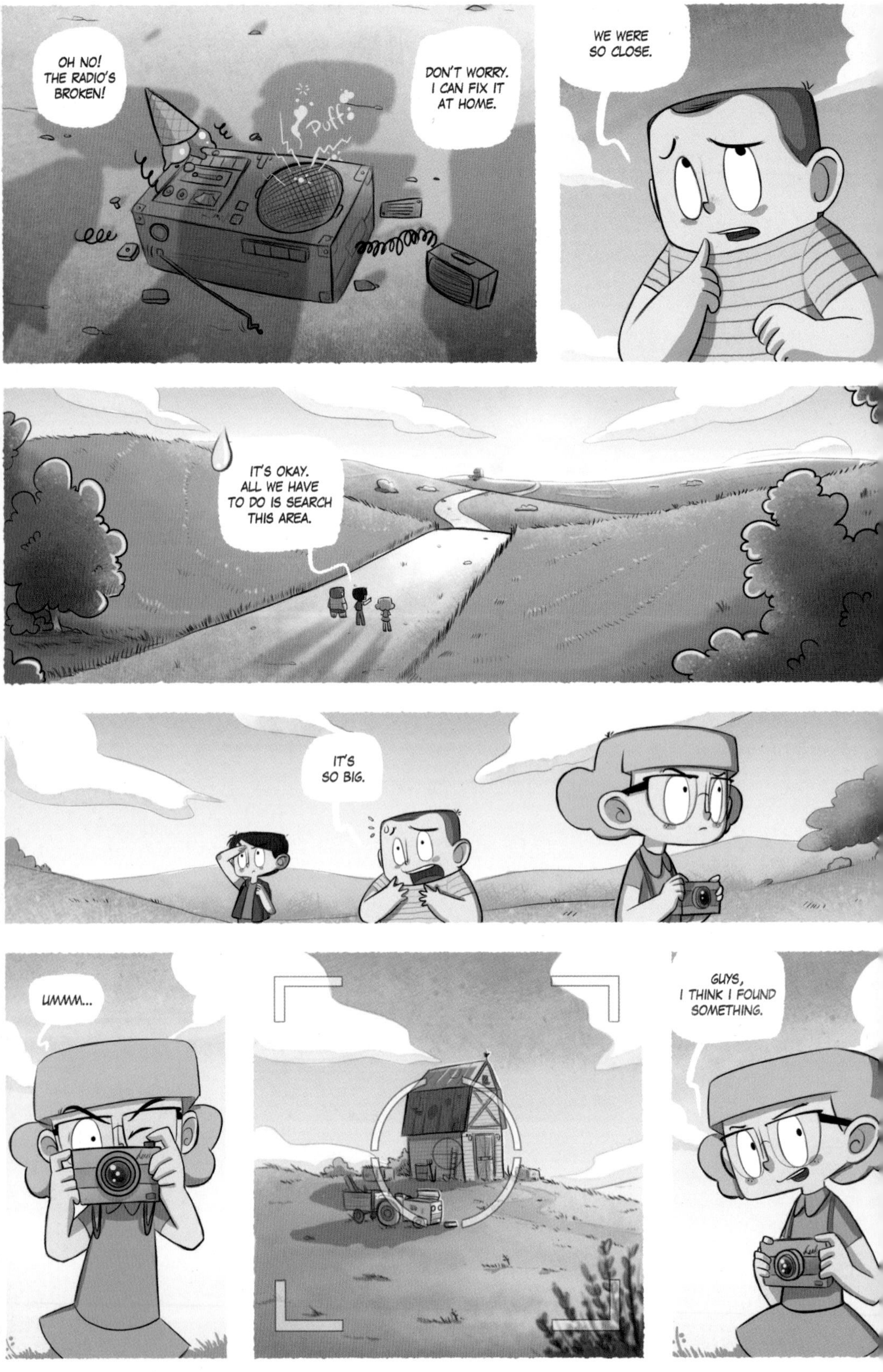
OH NO! THE RADIO'S BROKEN!
PUFF
DON'T WORRY. I CAN FIX IT AT HOME.
WE WERE SO CLOSE.
IT'S OKAY. ALL WE HAVE TO DO IS SEARCH THIS AREA.
IT'S SO BIG.
UMMM...
GUYS, I THINK I FOUND SOMETHING.

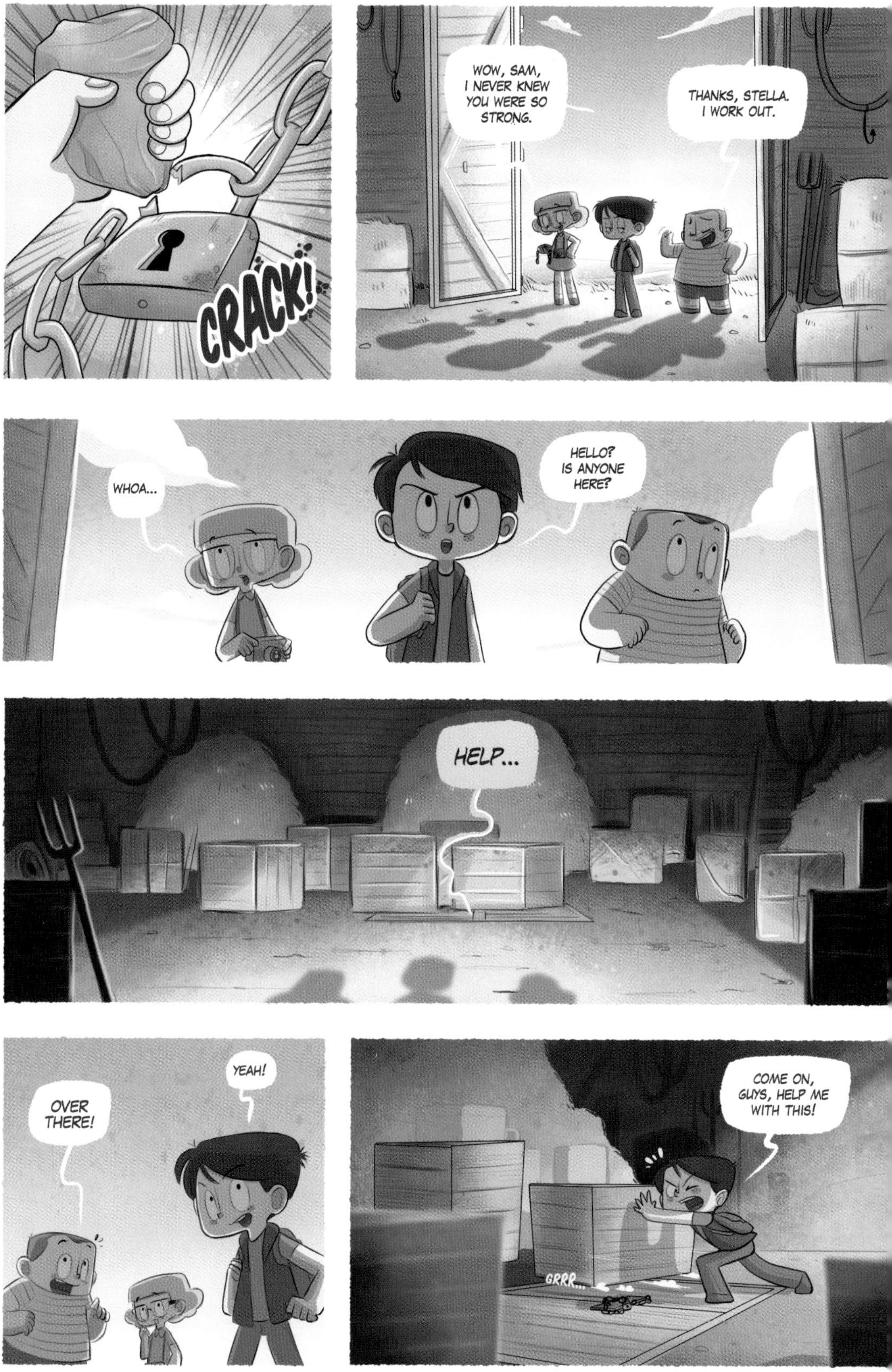
CRACK!
WOW, SAM, I NEVER KNEW YOU WERE SO STRONG.
THANKS, STELLA. I WORK OUT.
WHOA...
HELLO? IS ANYONE HERE?
HELP...
OVER THERE!
YEAH!
COME ON, GUYS, HELP ME WITH THIS!
GRRR...

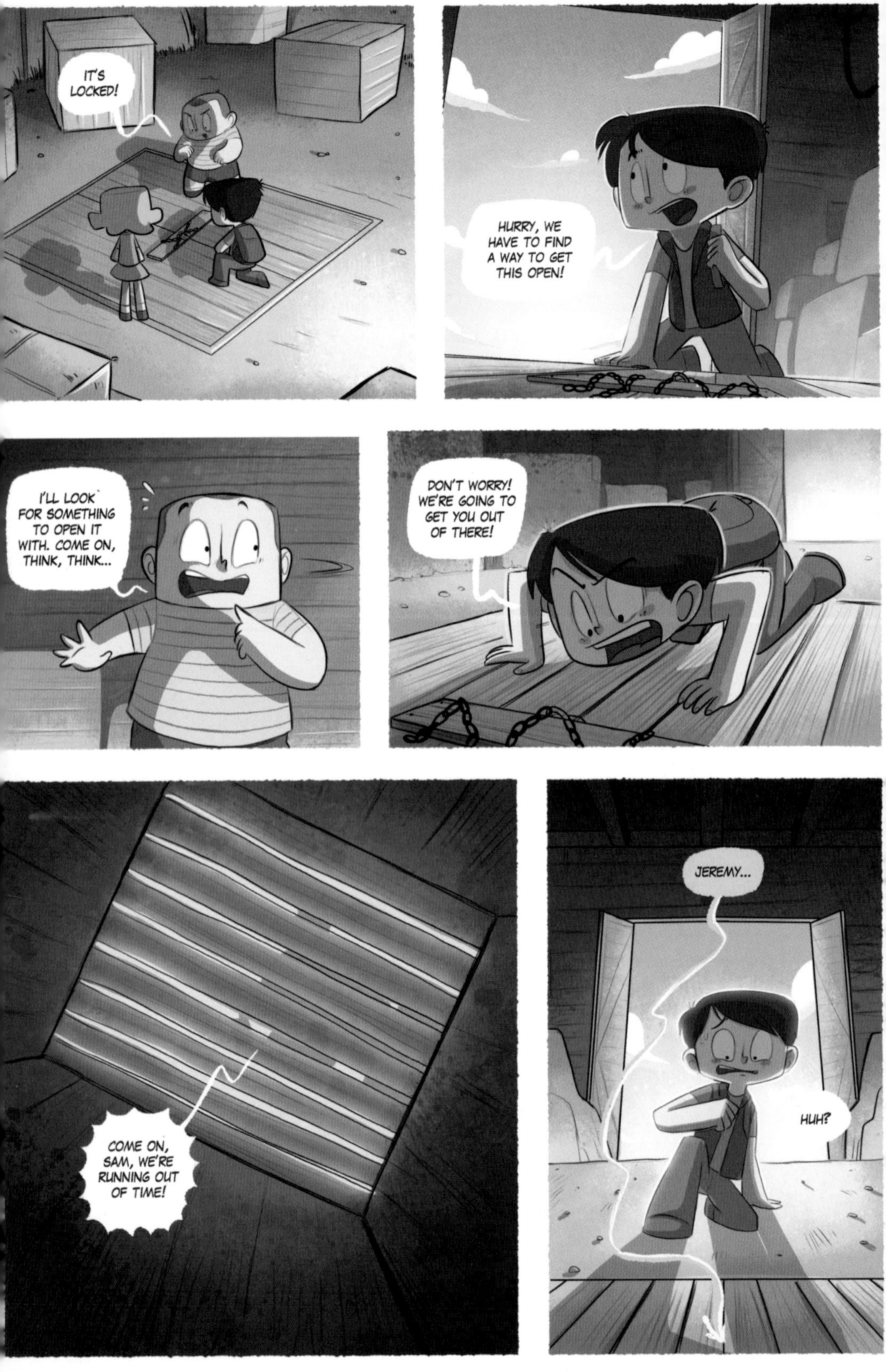
IT'S LOCKED!
HURRY, WE HAVE TO FIND A WAY TO GET THIS OPEN!
I'LL LOOK FOR SOMETHING TO OPEN IT WITH. COME ON, THINK, THINK...
DON'T WORRY! WE'RE GOING TO GET YOU OUT OF THERE!
COME ON, SAM, WE'RE RUNNING OUT OF TIME!
JEREMY...
HUH?

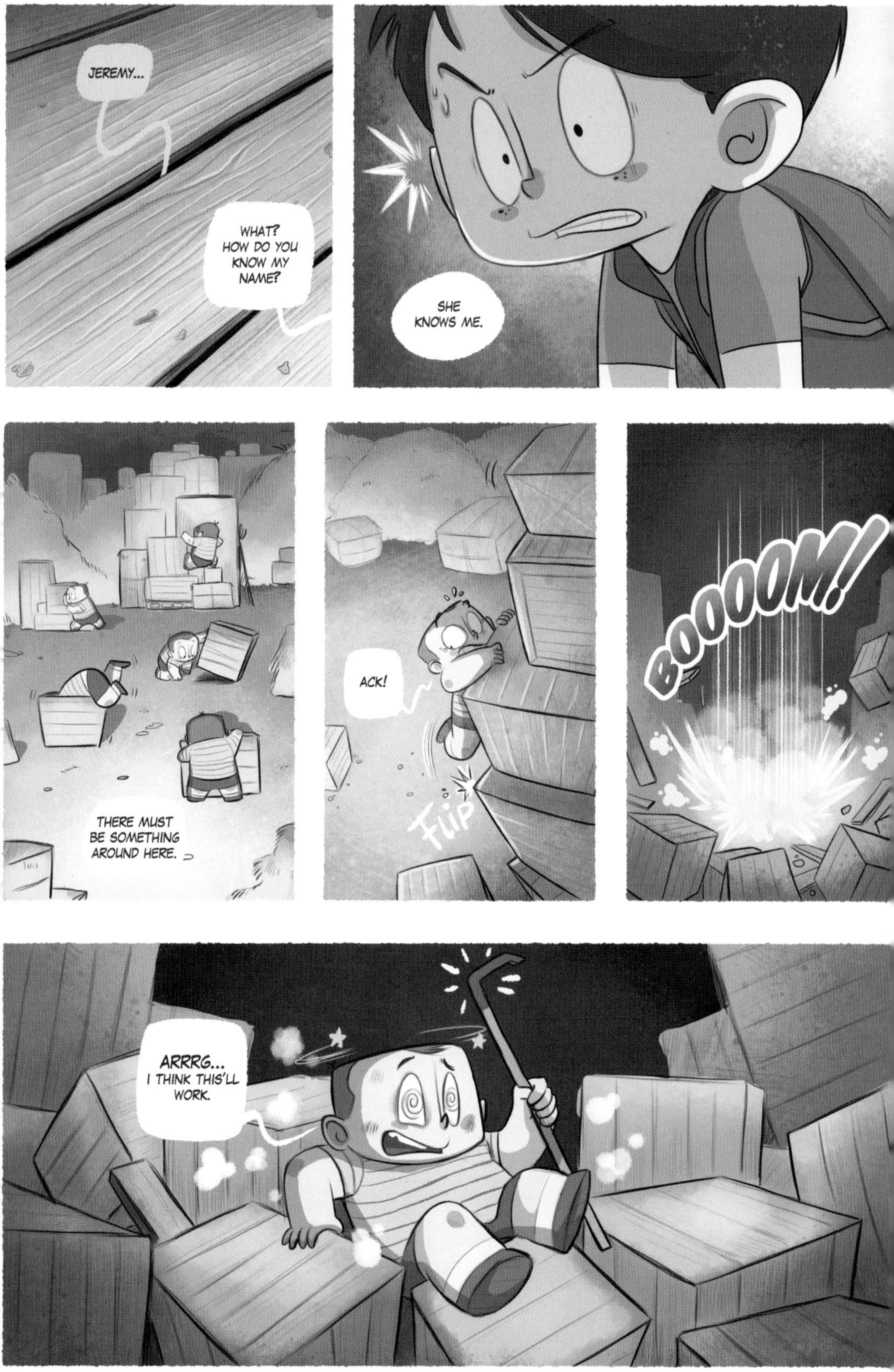
JEREMY...
WHAT? HOW DO YOU KNOW MY NAME?
SHE KNOWS ME.
THERE MUST BE SOMETHING AROUND HERE.
ACK!
FLIP
BOOOOM!!
ARRRG... I THINK THIS'LL WORK.

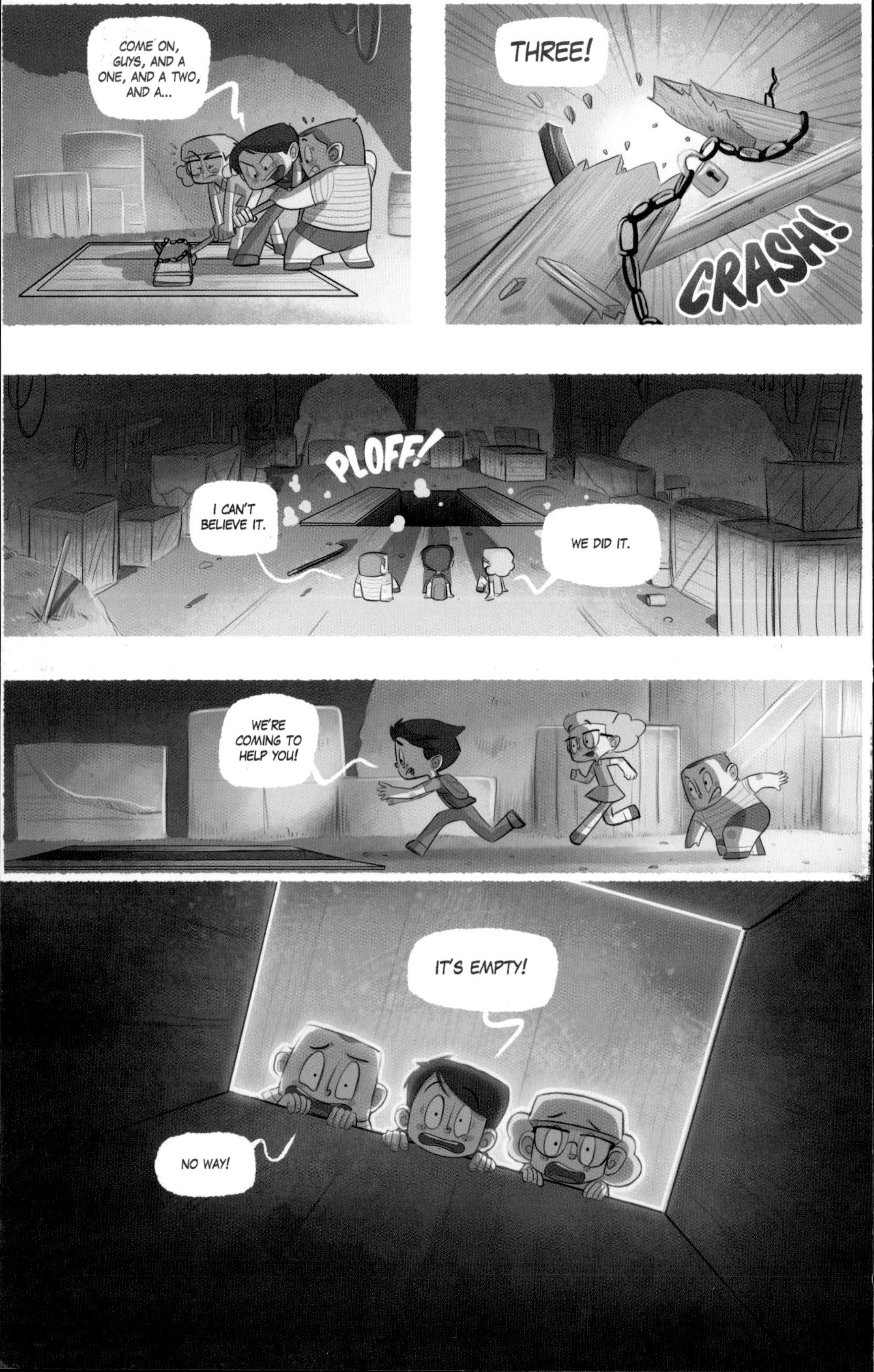
COME ON, GUYS, AND A ONE, AND A TWO, AND A...
THREE!
CRASH!
PLOFF!
I CAN'T BELIEVE IT.
WE DID IT.
WE'RE COMING TO HELP YOU!
IT'S EMPTY!
NO WAY!

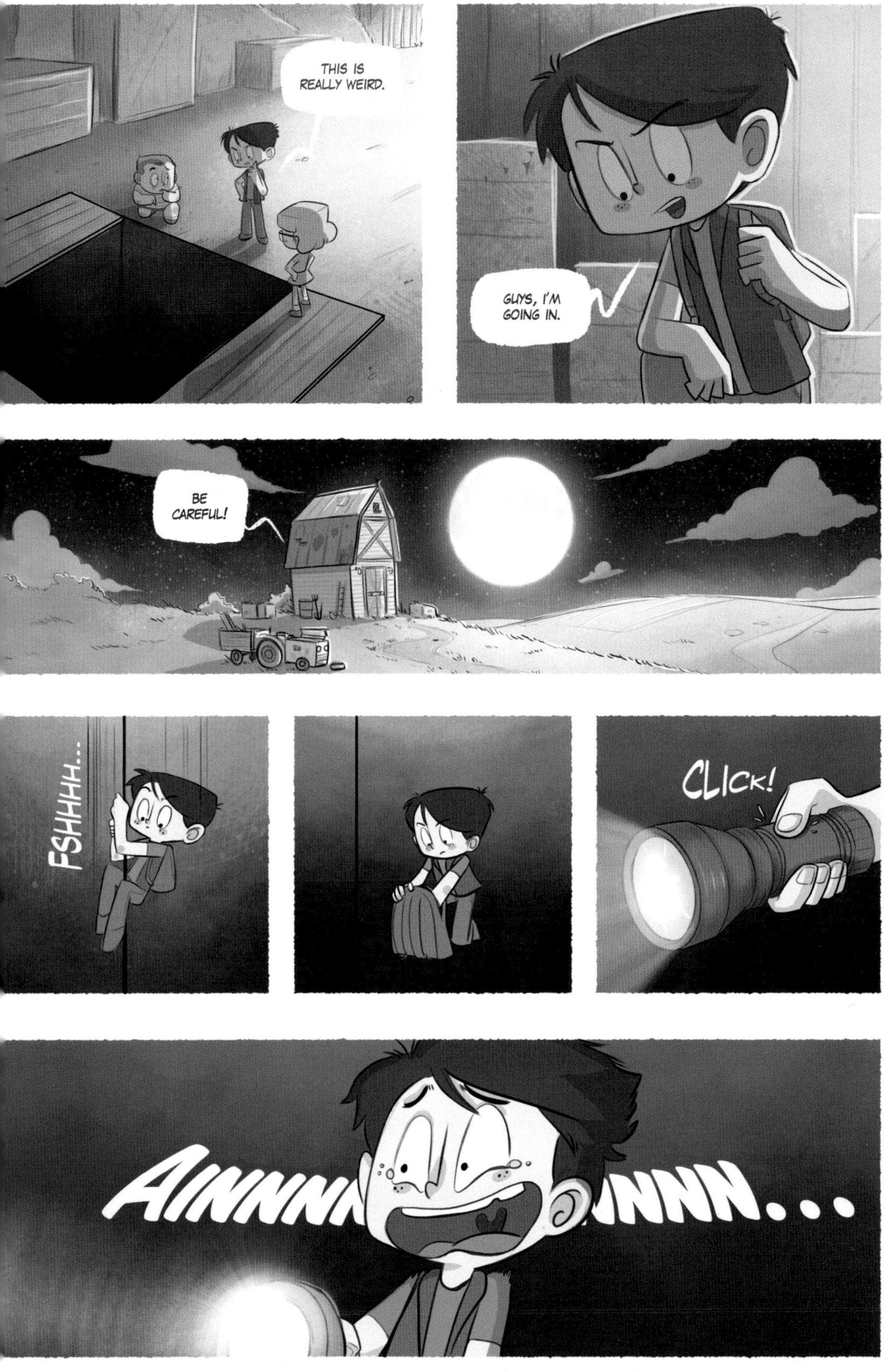
THIS IS REALLY WEIRD.
GUYS, I'M GOING IN.
BE CAREFUL!
FSHHHH...
CLICK!
AINNNNNNNNNNN...

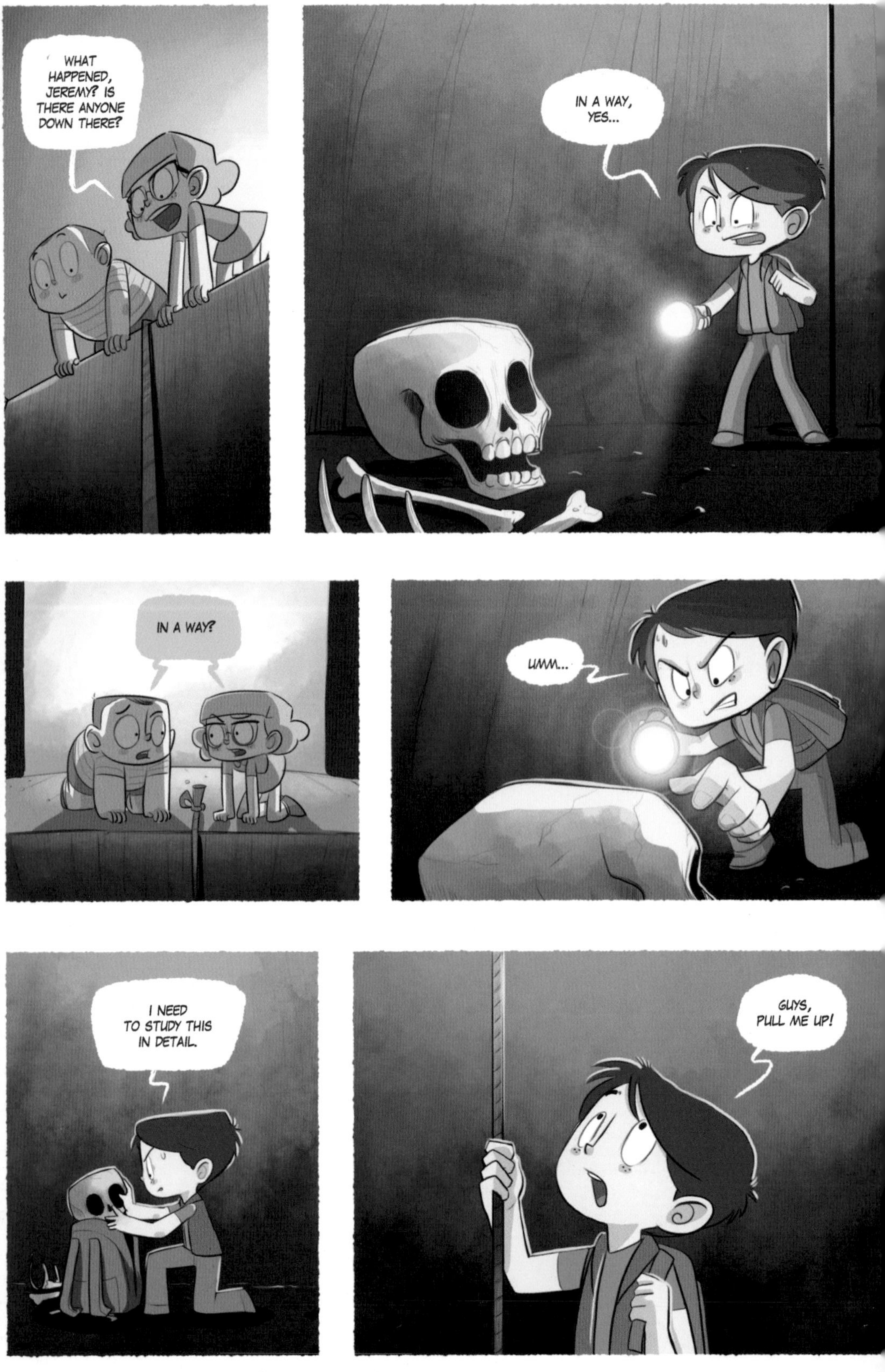
WHAT HAPPENED, JEREMY? IS THERE ANYONE DOWN THERE?
IN A WAY, YES...
IN A WAY?
UMM...
I NEED TO STUDY THIS IN DETAIL.
GUYS, PULL ME UP!

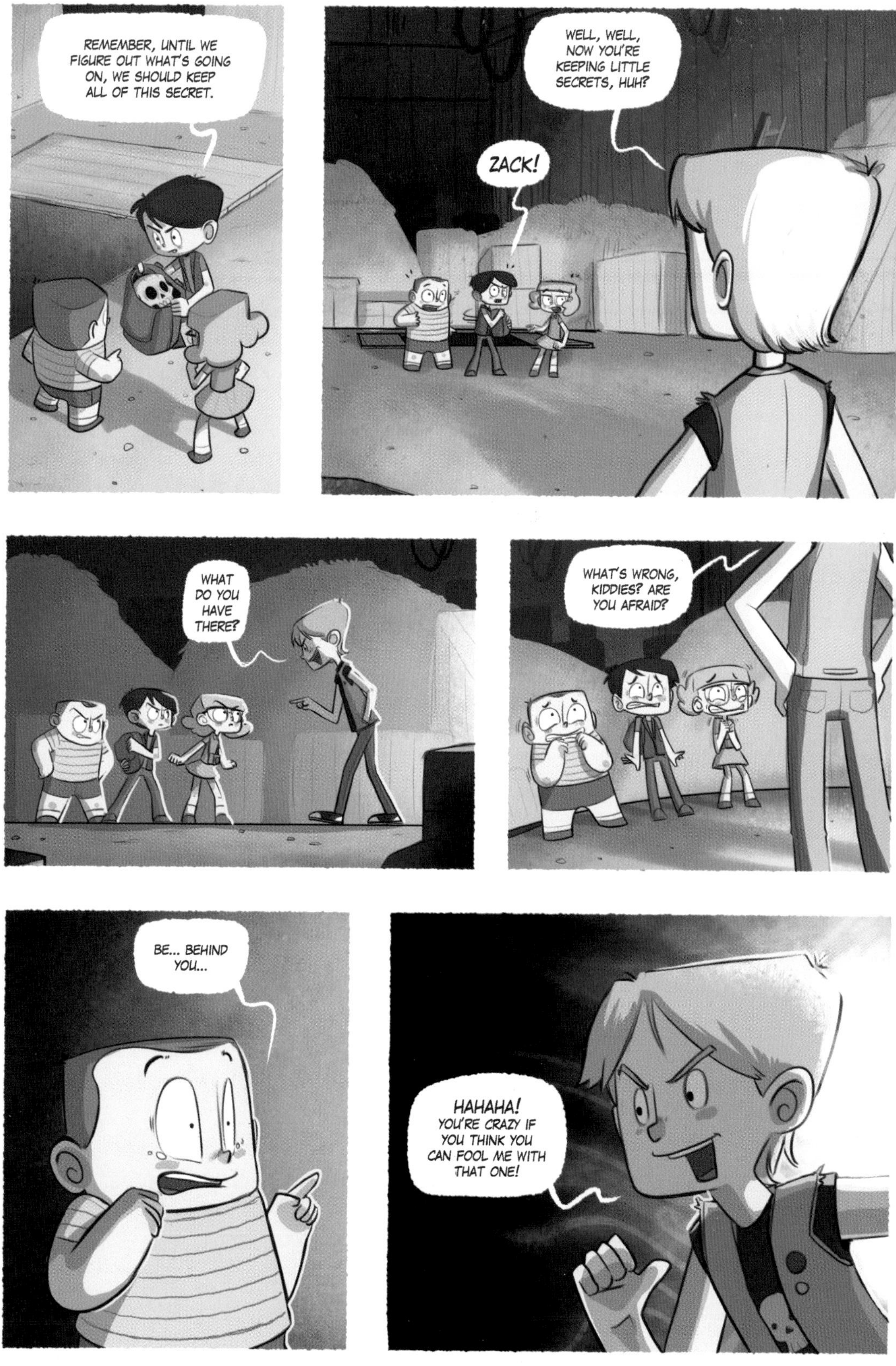
REMEMBER, UNTIL WE FIGURE OUT WHAT'S GOING ON, WE SHOULD KEEP ALL OF THIS SECRET.
WELL, WELL, NOW YOU'RE KEEPING LITTLE SECRETS, HUH?
ZACK!
WHAT DO YOU HAVE THERE?
WHAT'S WRONG, KIDDIES? ARE YOU AFRAID?
BE... BEHIND YOU...
HAHAHA! YOU'RE CRAZY IF YOU THINK YOU CAN FOOL ME WITH THAT ONE!

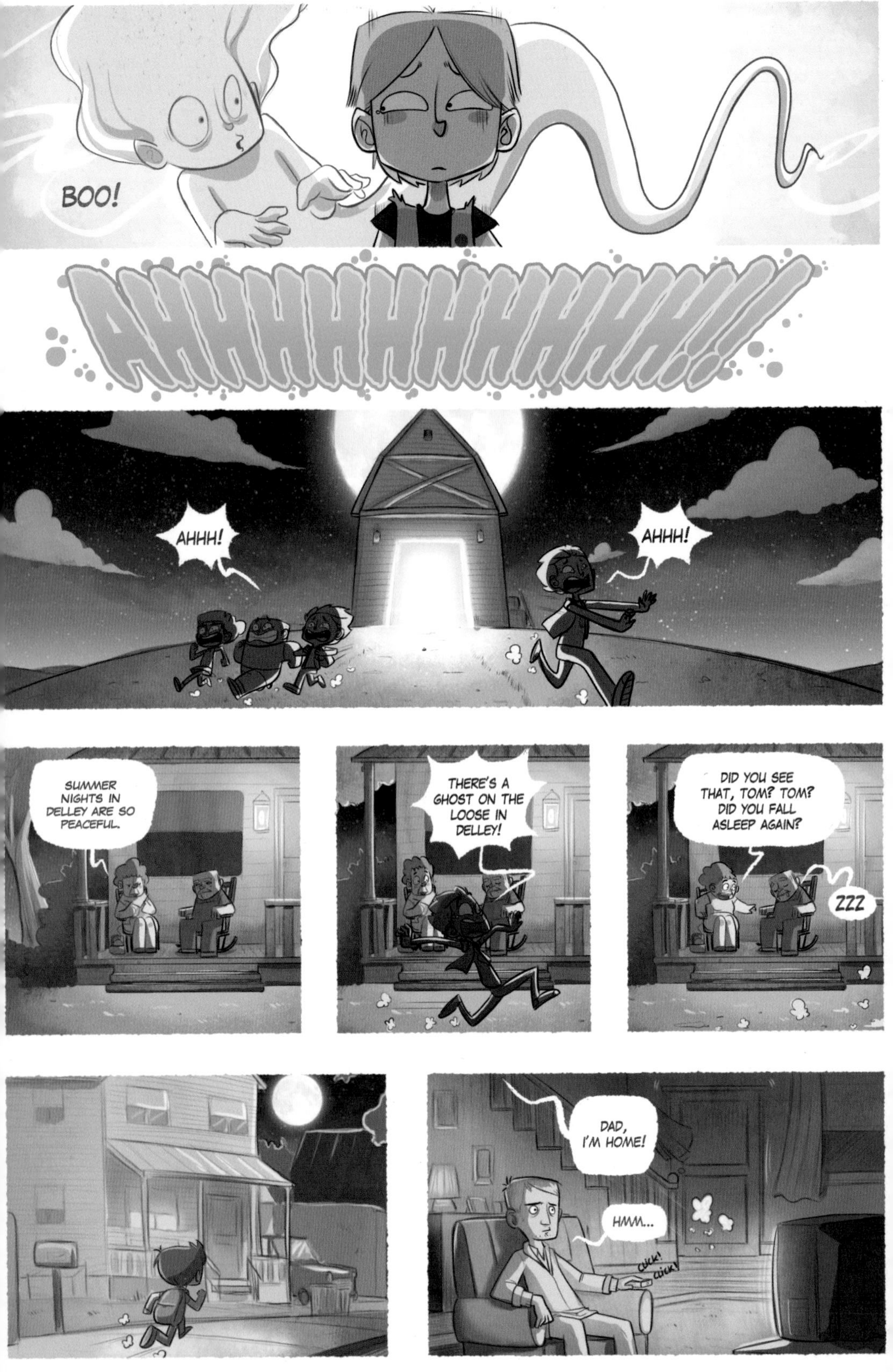
BOO!
AHHHHHHHHHHHH!!
AHHH!
AHHH!
SUMMER NIGHTS IN DELLEY ARE SO PEACEFUL.
THERE'S A GHOST ON THE LOOSE IN DELLEY!
DID YOU SEE THAT, TOM? TOM? DID YOU FALL ASLEEP AGAIN?
ZZZ
DAD, I'M HOME!
HMM...
CLICK! CLICK!

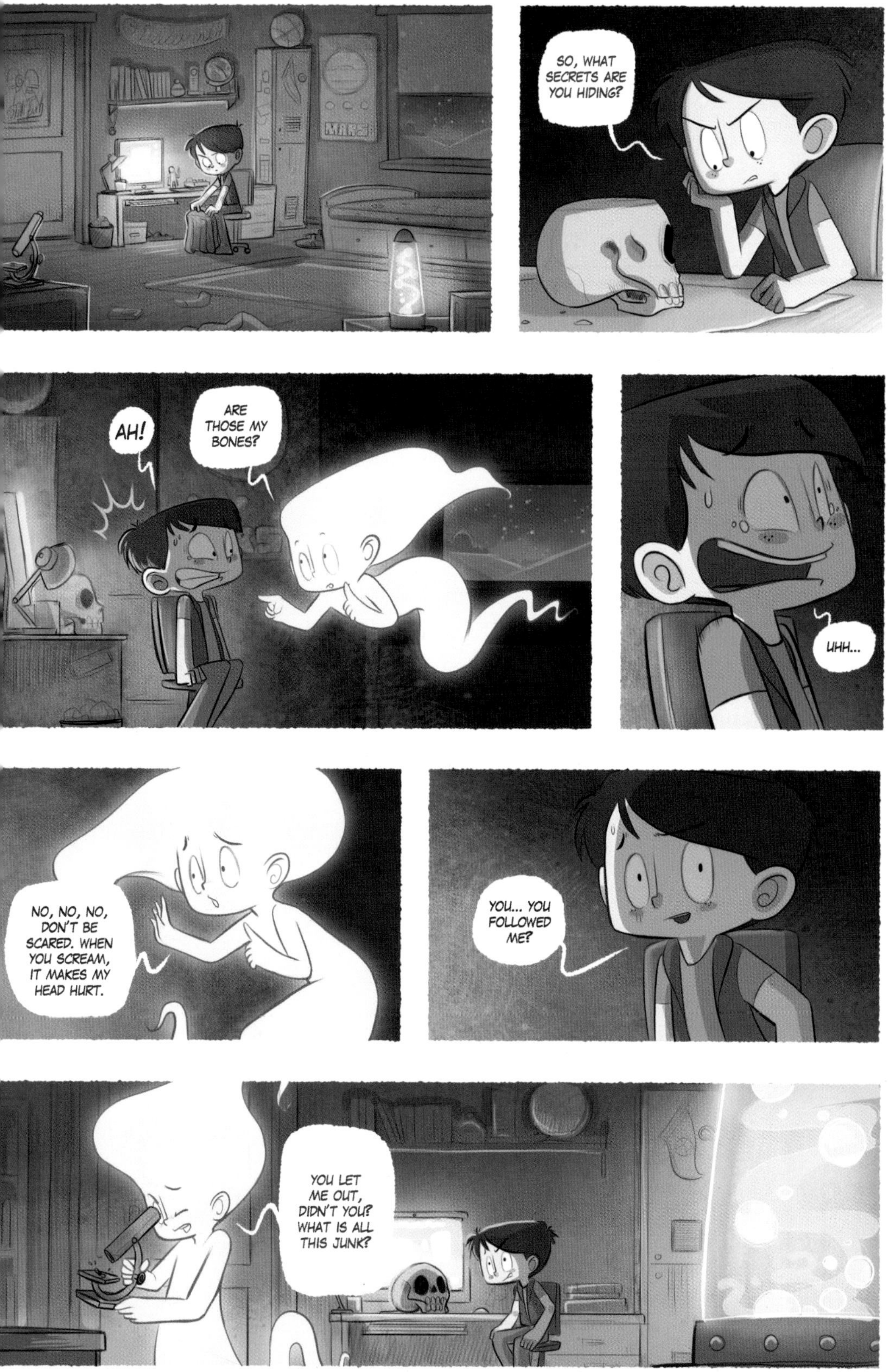
SO, WHAT SECRETS ARE YOU HIDING?
AH!
ARE THOSE MY BONES?
UHH...
NO, NO, NO, DON'T BE SCARED. WHEN YOU SCREAM, IT MAKES MY HEAD HURT.
YOU... YOU FOLLOWED ME?
YOU LET ME OUT, DIDN'T YOU? WHAT IS ALL THIS JUNK?

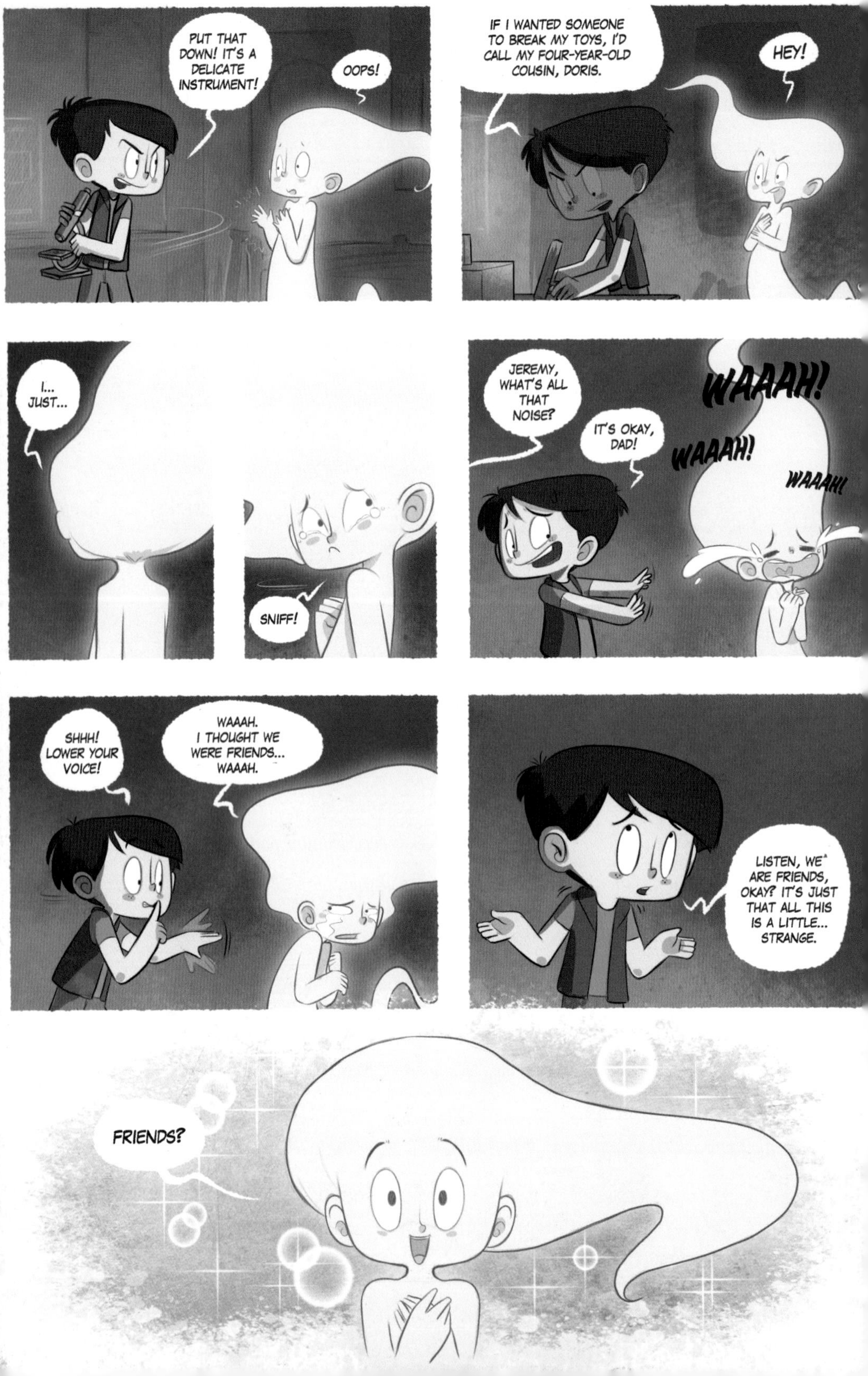
PUT THAT DOWN! IT'S A DELICATE INSTRUMENT!
OOPS!
IF I WANTED SOMEONE TO BREAK MY TOYS, I'D CALL MY FOUR-YEAR-OLD COUSIN, DORIS.
HEY!
I... JUST...
SNIFF!
JEREMY, WHAT'S ALL THAT NOISE?
IT'S OKAY, DAD!
WAAAH!
WAAAH!
WAAAH!
SHHH! LOWER YOUR VOICE!
WAAAH. I THOUGHT WE WERE FRIENDS... WAAAH.
LISTEN, WE ARE FRIENDS, OKAY? IT'S JUST THAT ALL THIS IS A LITTLE... STRANGE.
FRIENDS?

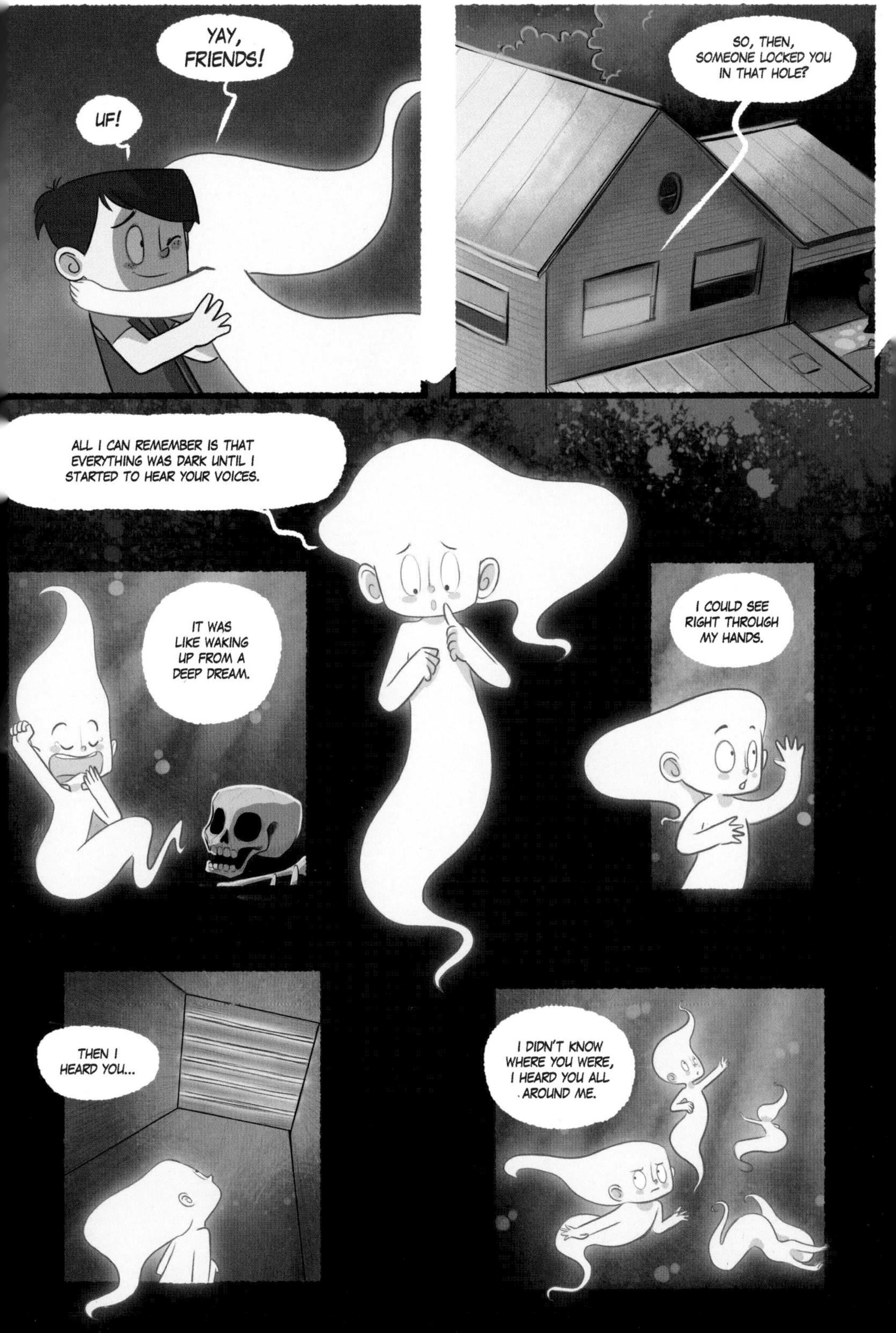
YAY, FRIENDS!
UF!
SO, THEN, SOMEONE LOCKED YOU IN THAT HOLE?
ALL I CAN REMEMBER IS THAT EVERYTHING WAS DARK UNTIL I STARTED TO HEAR YOUR VOICES.
IT WAS LIKE WAKING UP FROM A DEEP DREAM.
I COULD SEE RIGHT THROUGH MY HANDS.
THEN I HEARD YOU...
I DIDN'T KNOW WHERE YOU WERE, I HEARD YOU ALL AROUND ME.

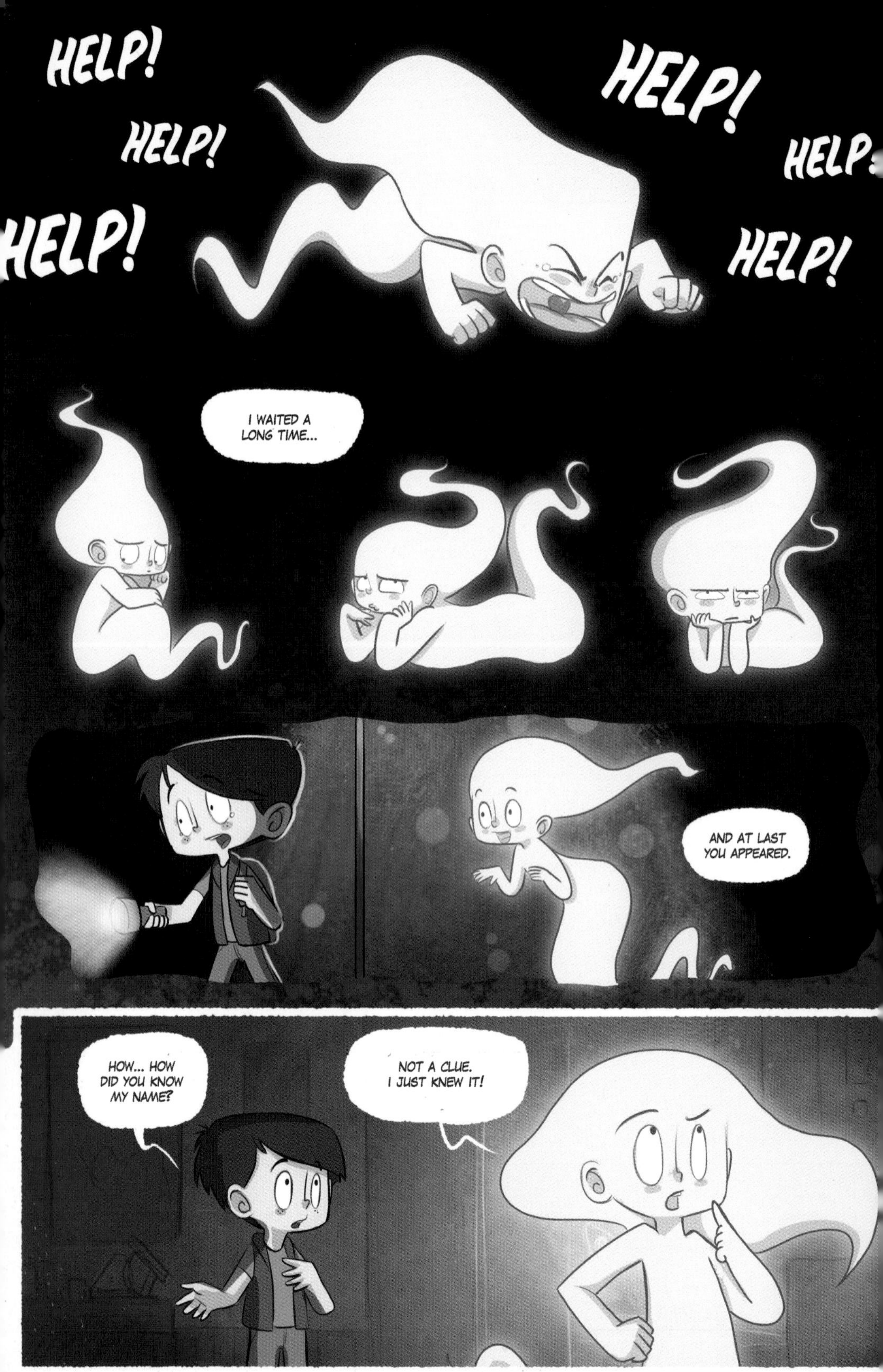
HELP!
HELP!
HELP!
HELP!
HELP!
HELP!
I WAITED A LONG TIME...
AND AT LAST YOU APPEARED.
HOW... HOW DID YOU KNOW MY NAME?
NOT A CLUE. I JUST KNEW IT!

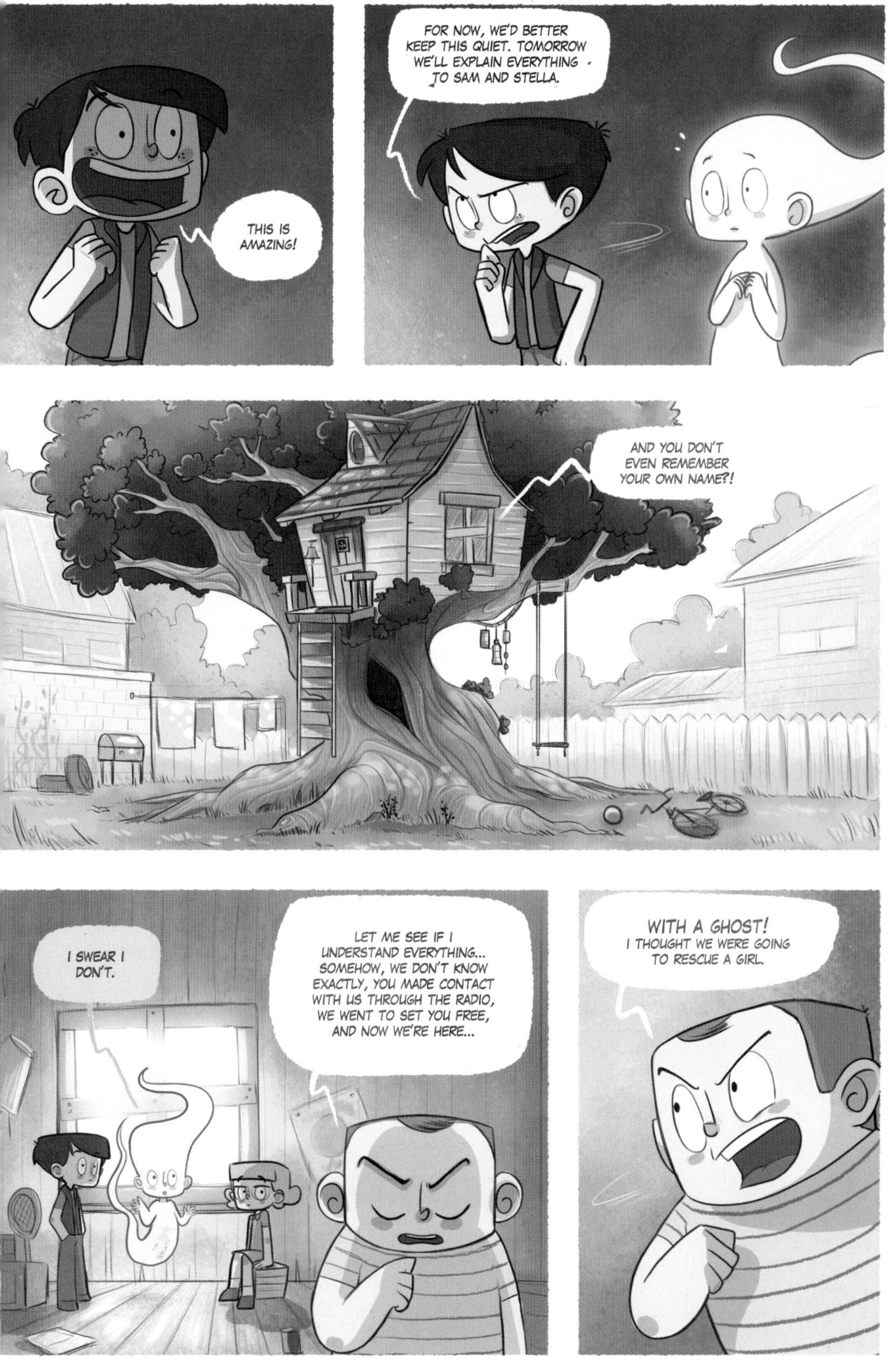
THIS IS AMAZING!
FOR NOW, WE'D BETTER KEEP THIS QUIET. TOMORROW WE'LL EXPLAIN EVERYTHING TO SAM AND STELLA.
AND YOU DON'T EVEN REMEMBER YOUR OWN NAME?!
I SWEAR I DON'T.
LET ME SEE IF I UNDERSTAND EVERYTHING... SOMEHOW, WE DON'T KNOW EXACTLY, YOU MADE CONTACT WITH US THROUGH THE RADIO, WE WENT TO SET YOU FREE, AND NOW WE'RE HERE...
WITH A GHOST! I THOUGHT WE WERE GOING TO RESCUE A GIRL.

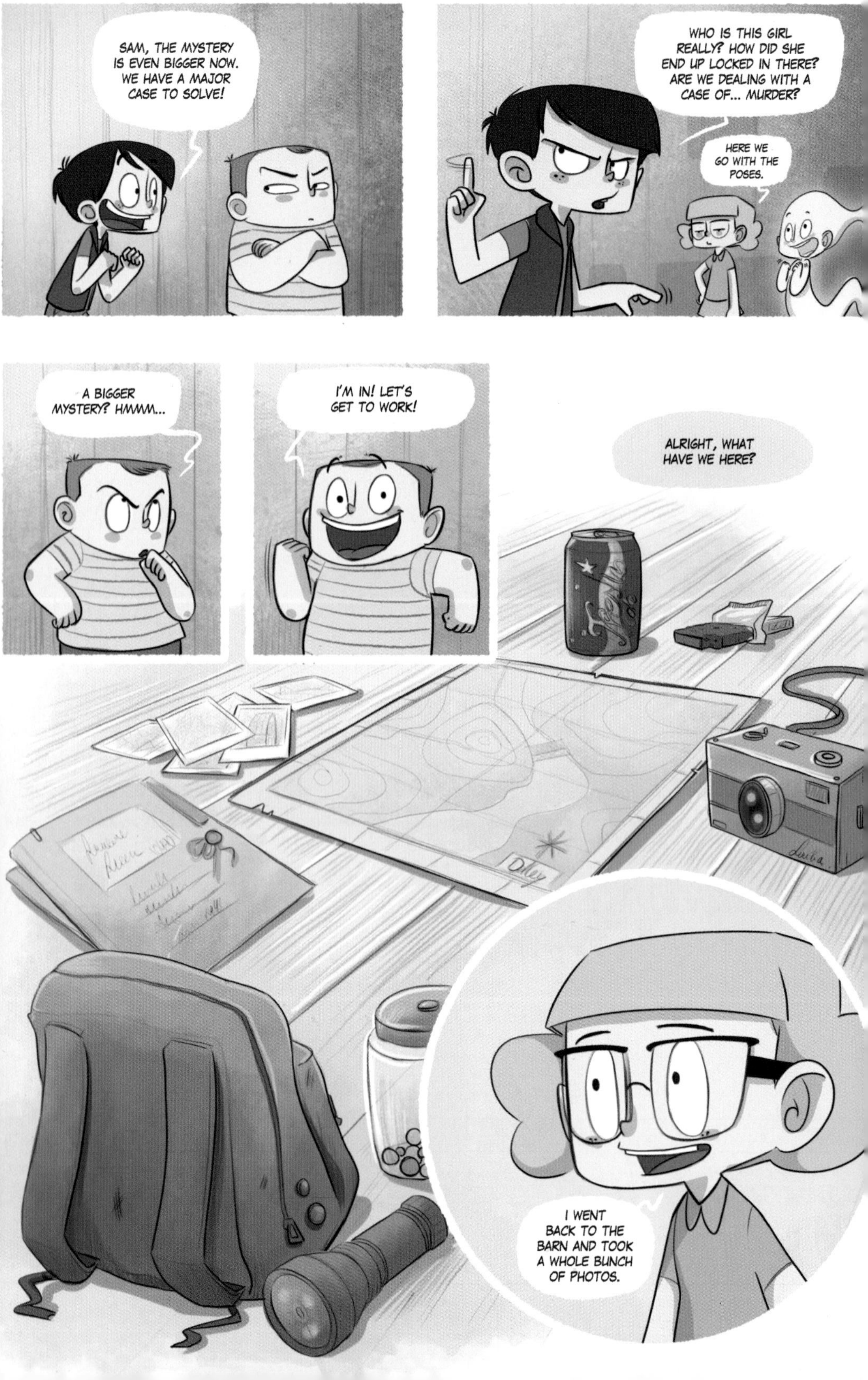
SAM, THE MYSTERY IS EVEN BIGGER NOW. WE HAVE A MAJOR CASE TO SOLVE!
WHO IS THIS GIRL REALLY? HOW DID SHE END UP LOCKED IN THERE? ARE WE DEALING WITH A CASE OF... MURDER?
HERE WE GO WITH THE POSES.
A BIGGER MYSTERY? HMMM...
I'M IN! LET'S GET TO WORK!
ALRIGHT, WHAT HAVE WE HERE?
I WENT BACK TO THE BARN AND TOOK A WHOLE BUNCH OF PHOTOS.

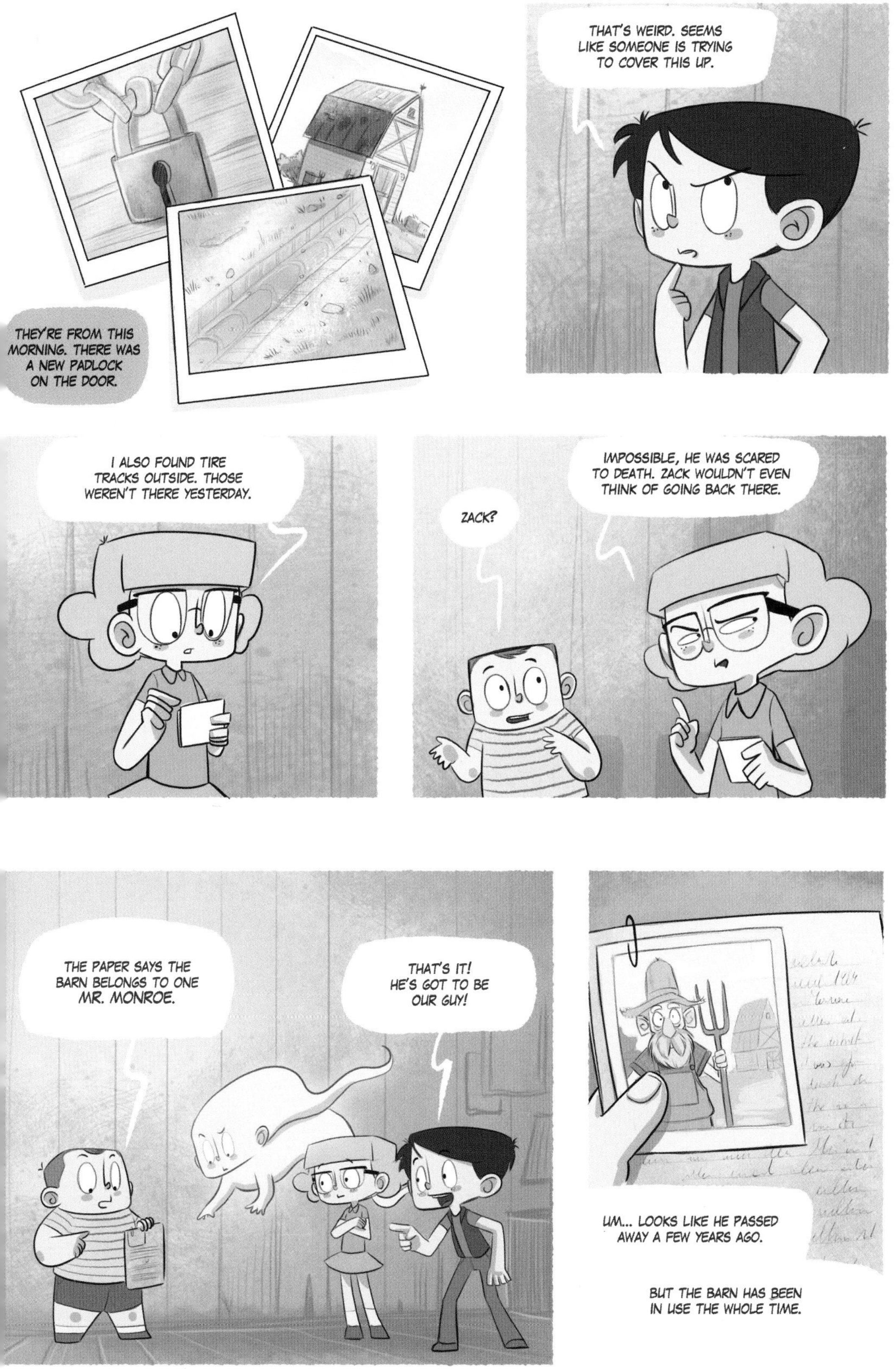
THEY'RE FROM THIS MORNING. THERE WAS A NEW PADLOCK ON THE DOOR.
THAT'S WEIRD. SEEMS LIKE SOMEONE IS TRYING TO COVER THIS UP.
I ALSO FOUND TIRE TRACKS OUTSIDE. THOSE WEREN'T THERE YESTERDAY.
ZACK?
IMPOSSIBLE, HE WAS SCARED TO DEATH. ZACK WOULDN'T EVEN THINK OF GOING BACK THERE.
THE PAPER SAYS THE BARN BELONGS TO ONE MR. MONROE.
THAT'S IT! HE'S GOT TO BE OUR GUY!
UM... LOOKS LIKE HE PASSED AWAY A FEW YEARS AGO.
BUT THE BARN HAS BEEN IN USE THE WHOLE TIME.

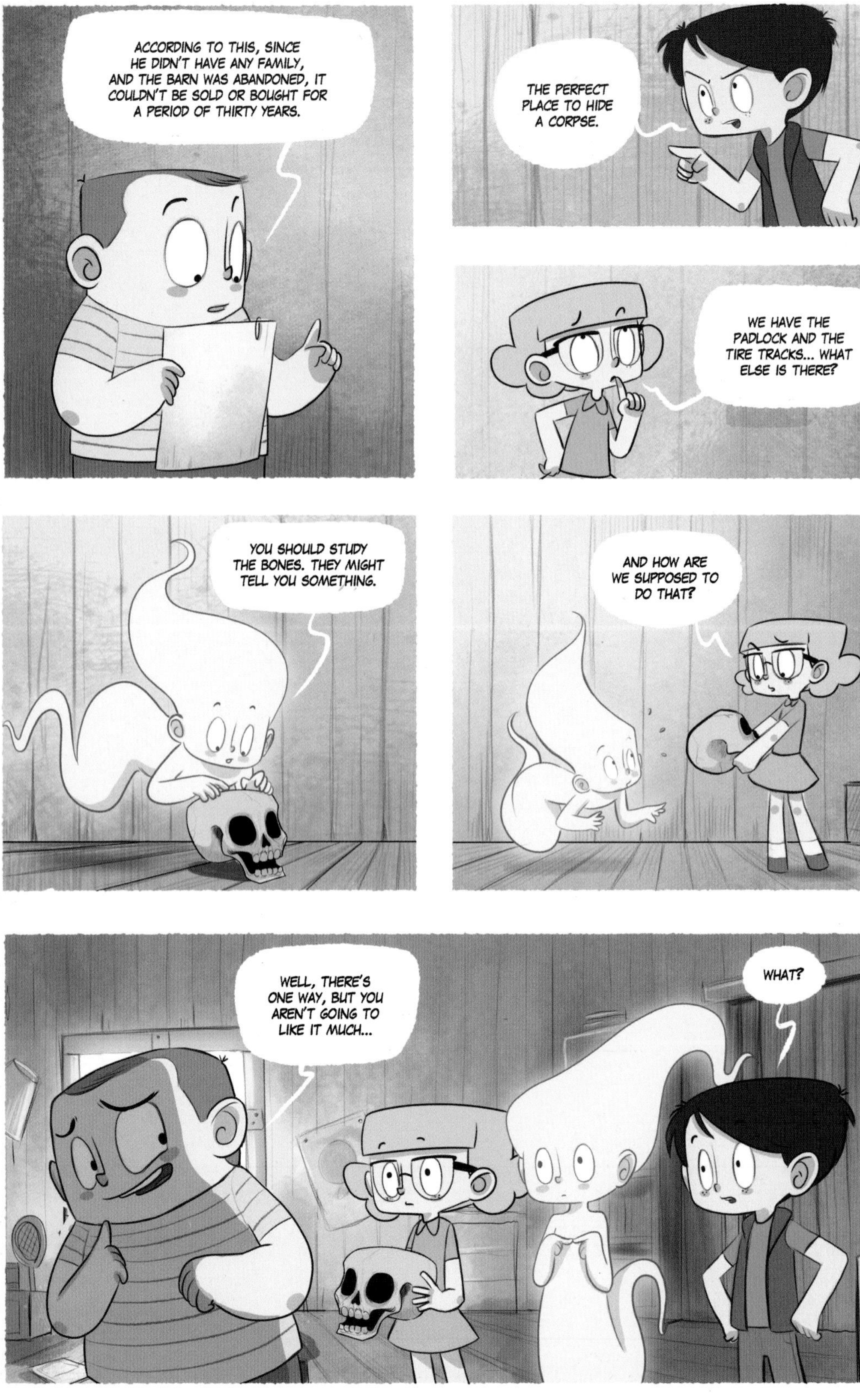
ACCORDING TO THIS, SINCE HE DIDN'T HAVE ANY FAMILY, AND THE BARN WAS ABANDONED, IT COULDN'T BE SOLD OR BOUGHT FOR A PERIOD OF THIRTY YEARS.
THE PERFECT PLACE TO HIDE A CORPSE.
WE HAVE THE PADLOCK AND THE TIRE TRACKS... WHAT ELSE IS THERE?
YOU SHOULD STUDY THE BONES. THEY MIGHT TELL YOU SOMETHING.
AND HOW ARE WE SUPPOSED TO DO THAT?
WELL, THERE'S ONE WAY, BUT YOU AREN'T GOING TO LIKE IT MUCH...
WHAT?

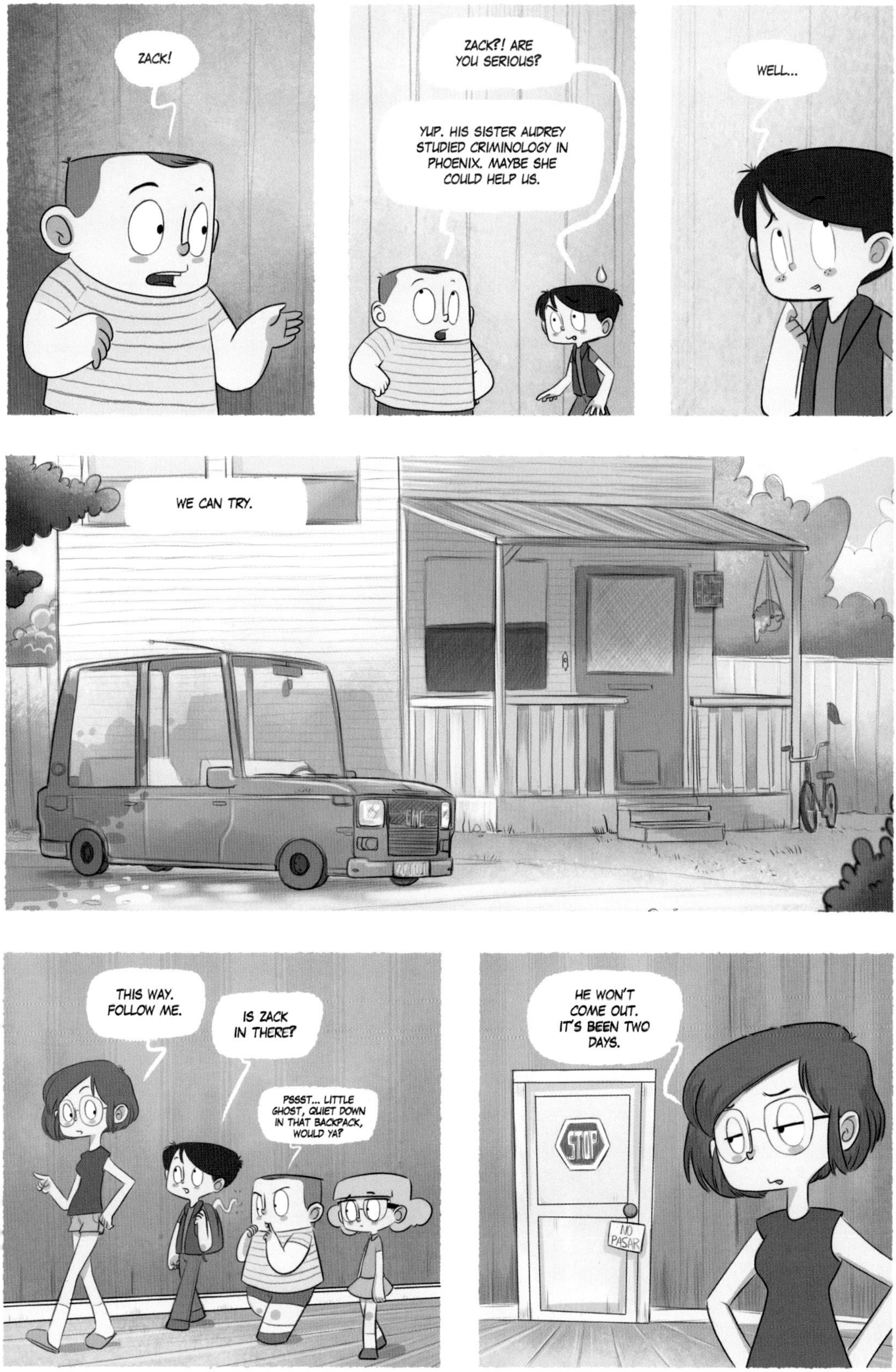
ZACK!
ZACK?! ARE YOU SERIOUS?
YUP. HIS SISTER AUDREY STUDIED CRIMINOLOGY IN PHOENIX. MAYBE SHE COULD HELP US.
WELL...
WE CAN TRY.
THIS WAY. FOLLOW ME.
IS ZACK IN THERE?
PSSST... LITTLE GHOST, QUIET DOWN IN THAT BACKPACK, WOULD YA?
HE WON'T COME OUT. IT'S BEEN TWO DAYS.
STOP
NO PASAR

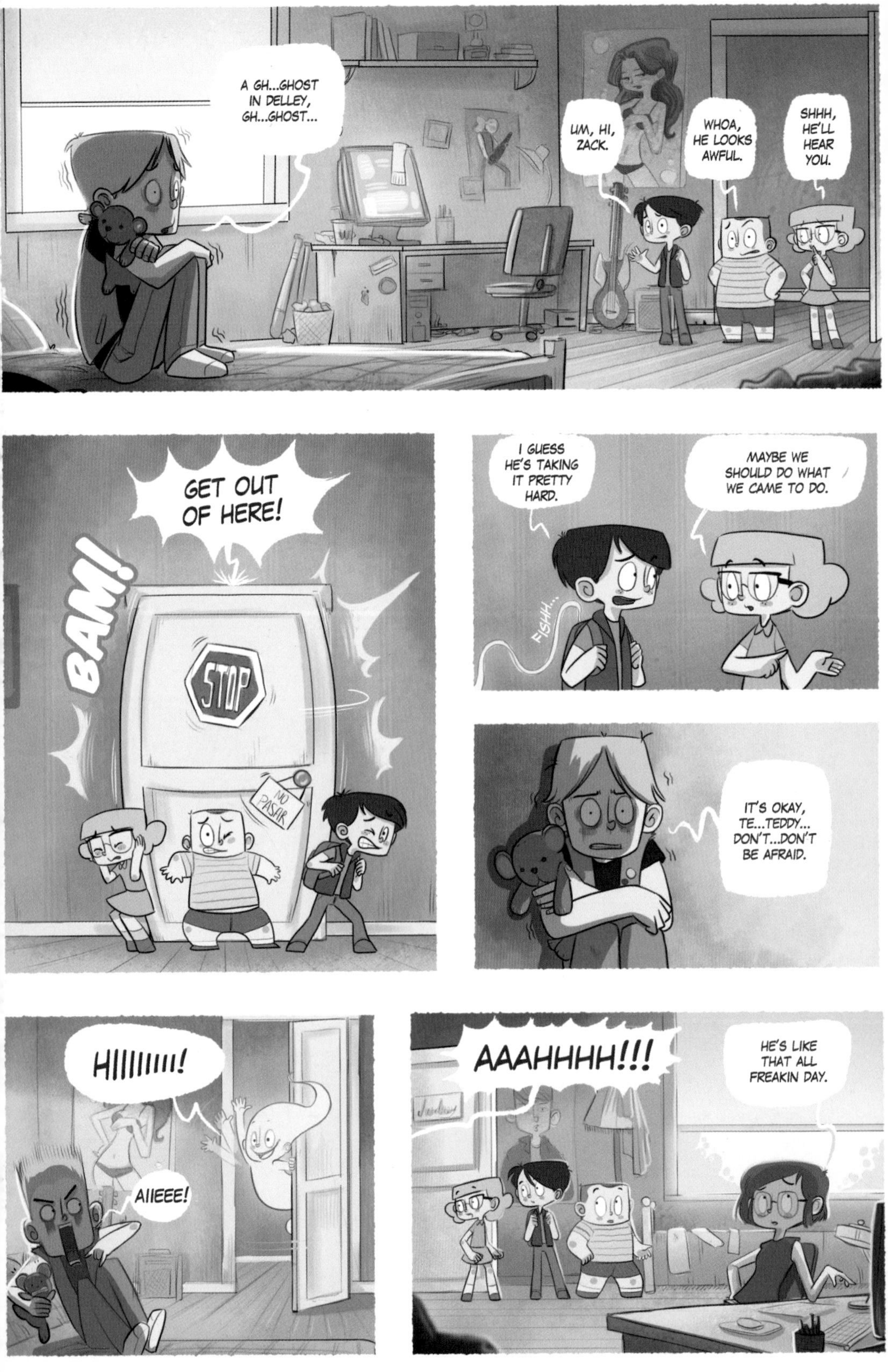
A GH...GHOST IN DELLEY, GH...GHOST...
UM, HI, ZACK.
WHOA, HE LOOKS AWFUL.
SHHH, HE'LL HEAR YOU.
GET OUT OF HERE!
BAM!
STOP
NO PASAR
I GUESS HE'S TAKING IT PRETTY HARD.
FISHH...
MAYBE WE SHOULD DO WHAT WE CAME TO DO.
IT'S OKAY, TE...TEDDY... DON'T...DON'T BE AFRAID.
HIIIIIIII!
AIIEEE!
AAAHHHH!!!
HE'S LIKE THAT ALL FREAKIN DAY.

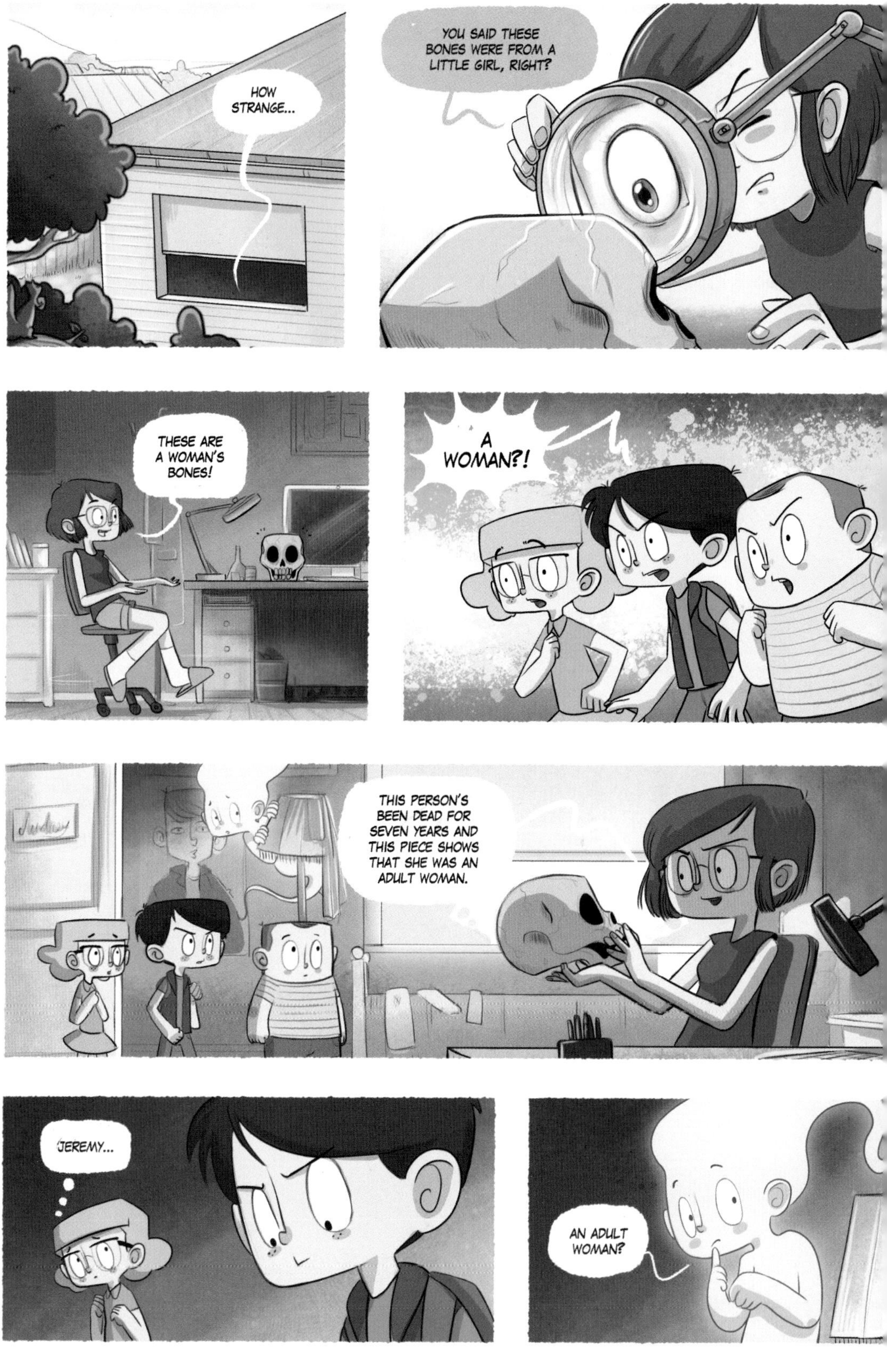
HOW STRANGE...
YOU SAID THESE BONES WERE FROM A LITTLE GIRL, RIGHT?
THESE ARE A WOMAN'S BONES!
A WOMAN?!
THIS PERSON'S BEEN DEAD FOR SEVEN YEARS AND THIS PIECE SHOWS THAT SHE WAS AN ADULT WOMAN.
JEREMY...
AN ADULT WOMAN?

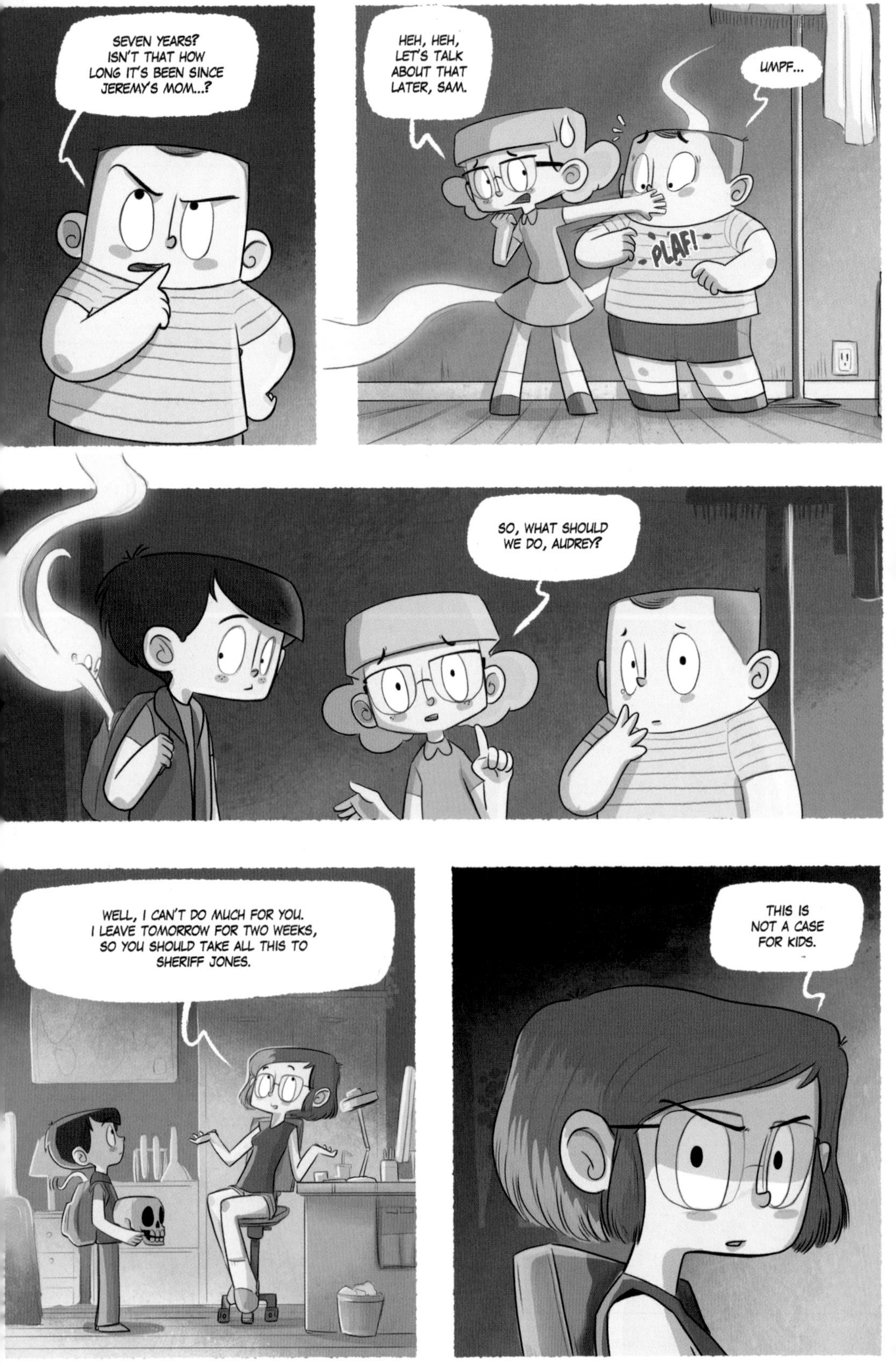
SEVEN YEARS? ISN'T THAT HOW LONG IT'S BEEN SINCE JEREMY'S MOM...?
HEH, HEH, LET'S TALK ABOUT THAT LATER, SAM.
UMPF...
PLAF!
SO, WHAT SHOULD WE DO, AUDREY?
WELL, I CAN'T DO MUCH FOR YOU. I LEAVE TOMORROW FOR TWO WEEKS, SO YOU SHOULD TAKE ALL THIS TO SHERIFF JONES.
THIS IS NOT A CASE FOR KIDS.

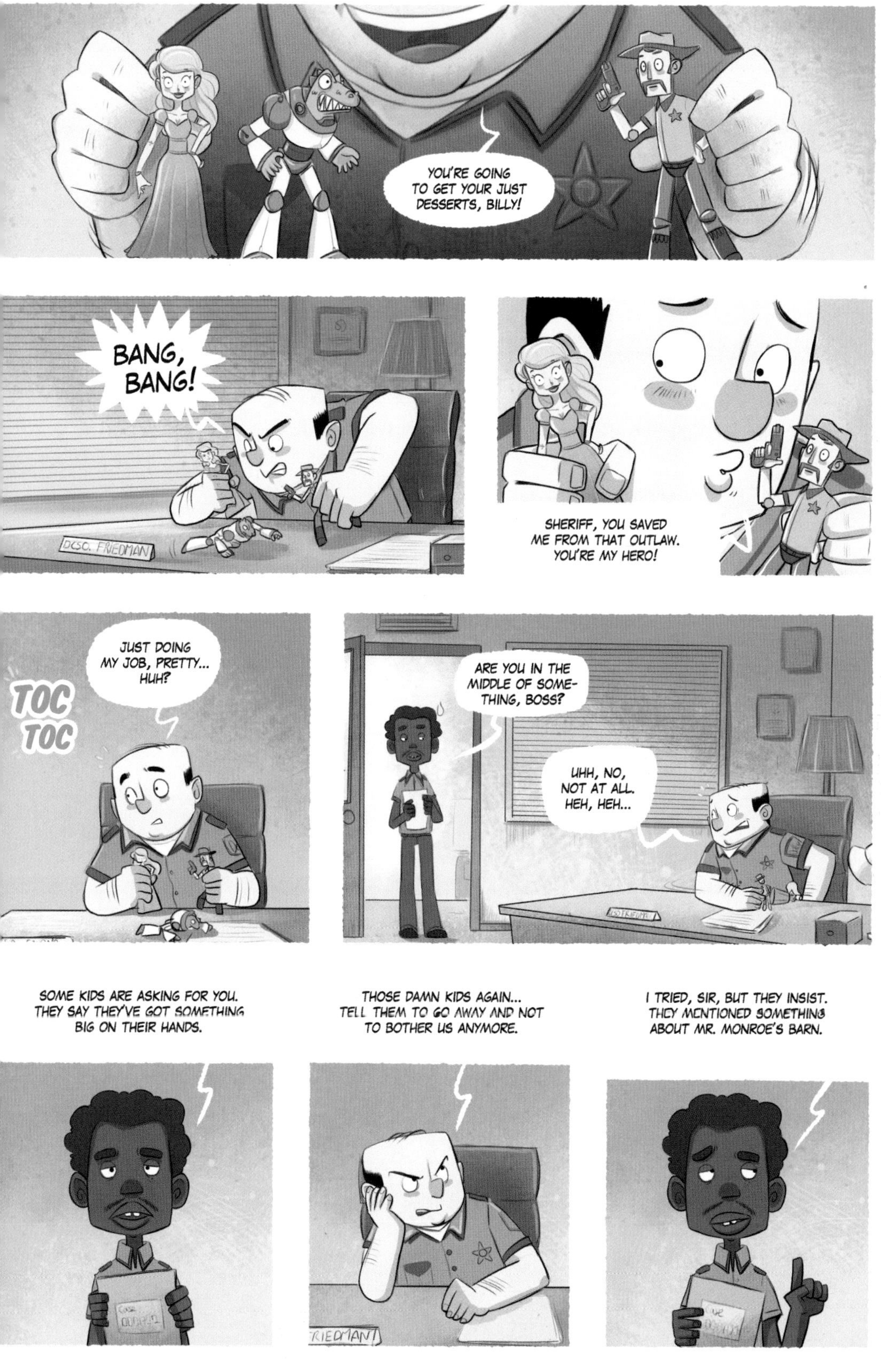
YOU'RE GOING TO GET YOUR JUST DESSERTS, BILLY!
BANG, BANG!
DCSO. FRIEDMAN
SHERIFF, YOU SAVED ME FROM THAT OUTLAW. YOU'RE MY HERO!
JUST DOING MY JOB, PRETTY... HUH?
TOC TOC
ARE YOU IN THE MIDDLE OF SOME-THING, BOSS?
UHH, NO, NOT AT ALL. HEH, HEH...
SOME KIDS ARE ASKING FOR YOU. THEY SAY THEY'VE GOT SOMETHING BIG ON THEIR HANDS.
THOSE DAMN KIDS AGAIN... TELL THEM TO GO AWAY AND NOT TO BOTHER US ANYMORE.
I TRIED, SIR, BUT THEY INSIST. THEY MENTIONED SOMETHING ABOUT MR. MONROE'S BARN.
FRIEDMAN

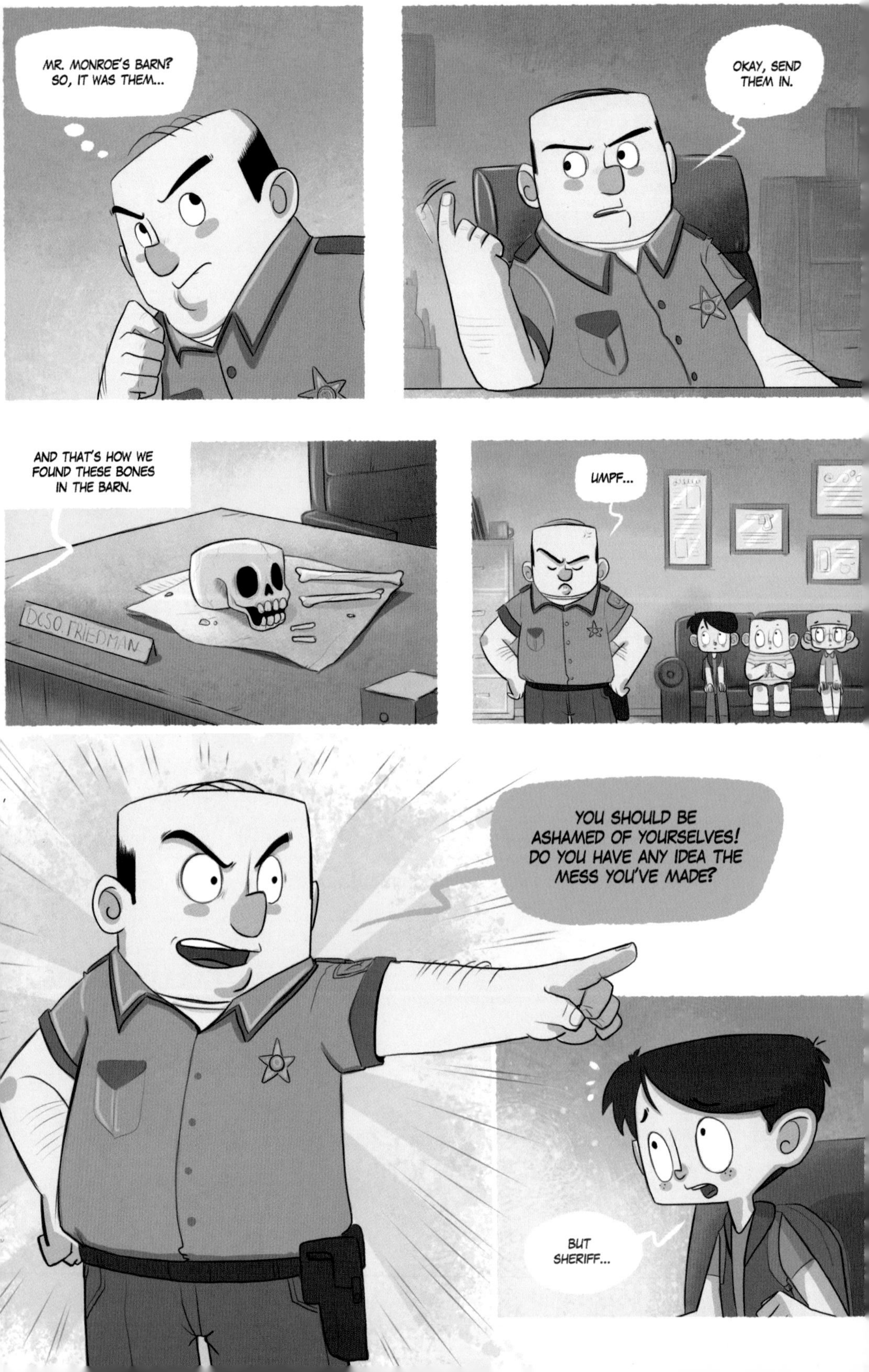
MR. MONROE'S BARN? SO, IT WAS THEM...
OKAY, SEND THEM IN.
AND THAT'S HOW WE FOUND THESE BONES IN THE BARN.
DCSO. FRIEDMAN
UMPF...
YOU SHOULD BE ASHAMED OF YOURSELVES! DO YOU HAVE ANY IDEA THE MESS YOU'VE MADE?
BUT SHERIFF...

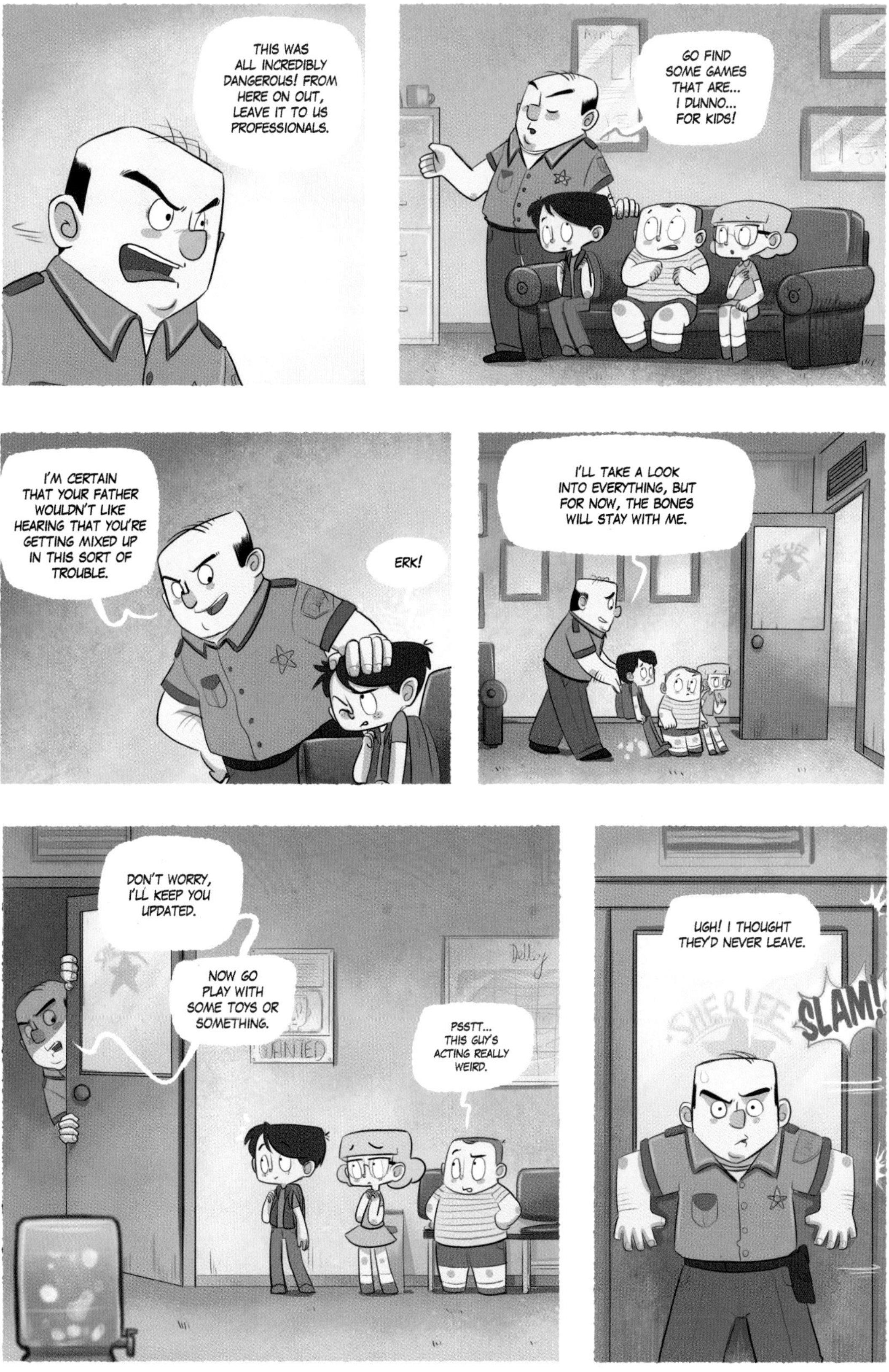
THIS WAS ALL INCREDIBLY DANGEROUS! FROM HERE ON OUT, LEAVE IT TO US PROFESSIONALS.
GO FIND SOME GAMES THAT ARE... I DUNNO... FOR KIDS!
I'M CERTAIN THAT YOUR FATHER WOULDN'T LIKE HEARING THAT YOU'RE GETTING MIXED UP IN THIS SORT OF TROUBLE.
ERK!
I'LL TAKE A LOOK INTO EVERYTHING, BUT FOR NOW, THE BONES WILL STAY WITH ME.
DON'T WORRY, I'LL KEEP YOU UPDATED.
NOW GO PLAY WITH SOME TOYS OR SOMETHING.
WANTED
PSSTT... THIS GUY'S ACTING REALLY WEIRD.
UGH! I THOUGHT THEY'D NEVER LEAVE.
SHERIFF
SLAM!

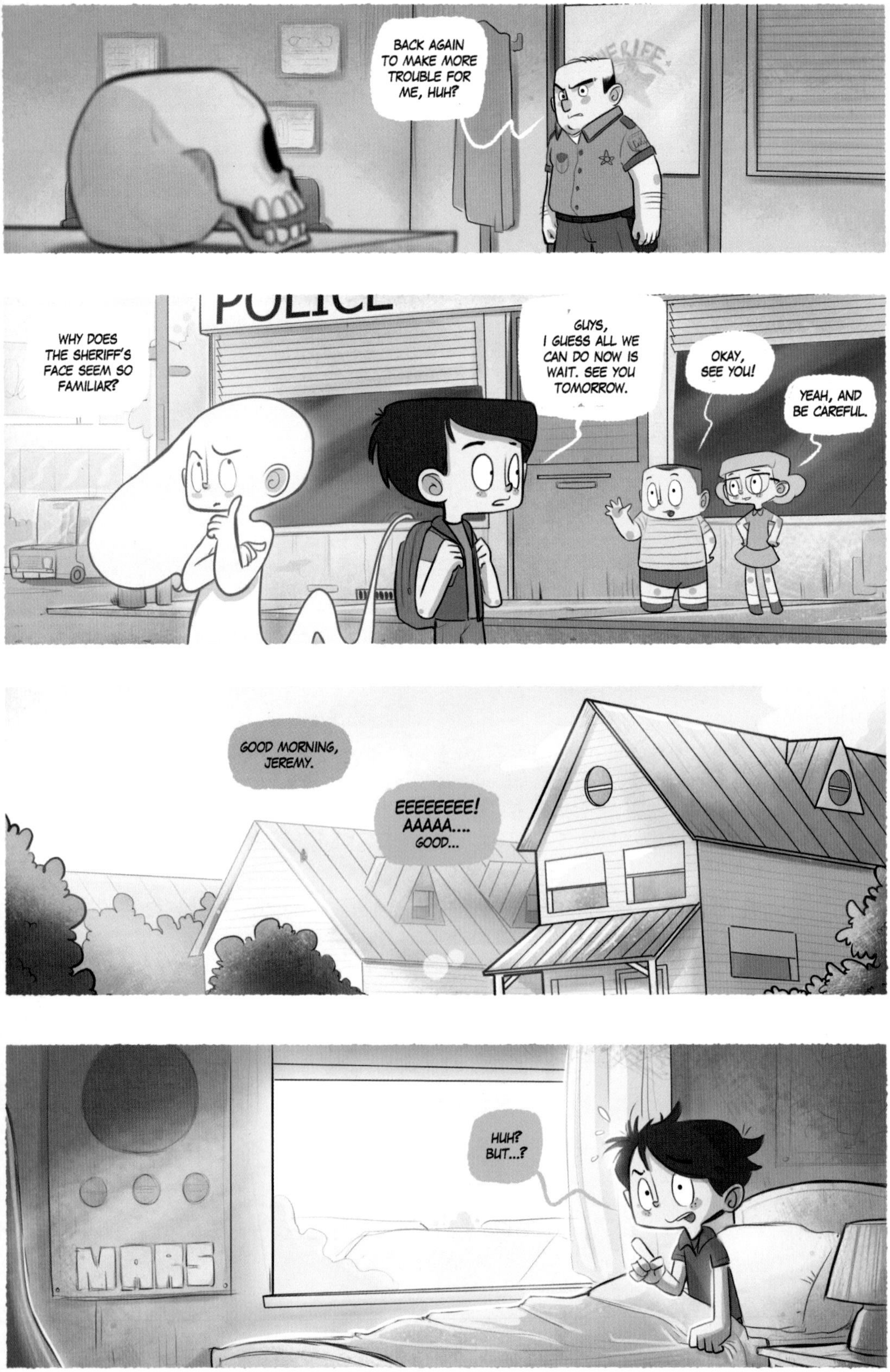
BACK AGAIN TO MAKE MORE TROUBLE FOR ME, HUH?
POLICE
WHY DOES THE SHERIFF'S FACE SEEM SO FAMILIAR?
GUYS, I GUESS ALL WE CAN DO NOW IS WAIT. SEE YOU TOMORROW.
OKAY, SEE YOU!
YEAH, AND BE CAREFUL.
GOOD MORNING, JEREMY.
EEEEEEEE! AAAAA.... GOOD...
MARS
HUH? BUT...?

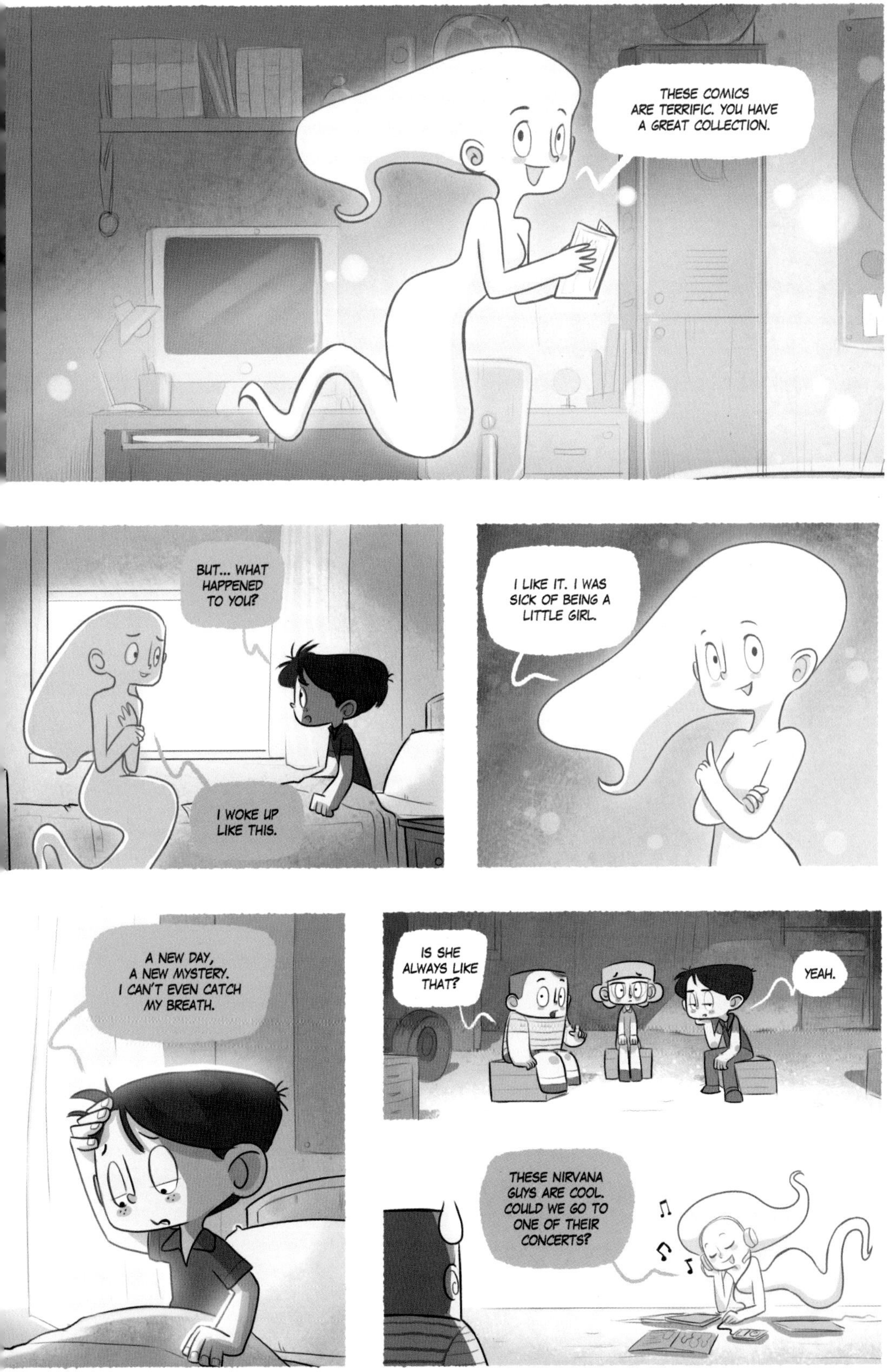
THESE COMICS ARE TERRIFIC. YOU HAVE A GREAT COLLECTION.
BUT... WHAT HAPPENED TO YOU?
I WOKE UP LIKE THIS.
I LIKE IT. I WAS SICK OF BEING A LITTLE GIRL.
A NEW DAY, A NEW MYSTERY. I CAN'T EVEN CATCH MY BREATH.
IS SHE ALWAYS LIKE THAT?
YEAH.
THESE NIRVANA GUYS ARE COOL. COULD WE GO TO ONE OF THEIR CONCERTS?

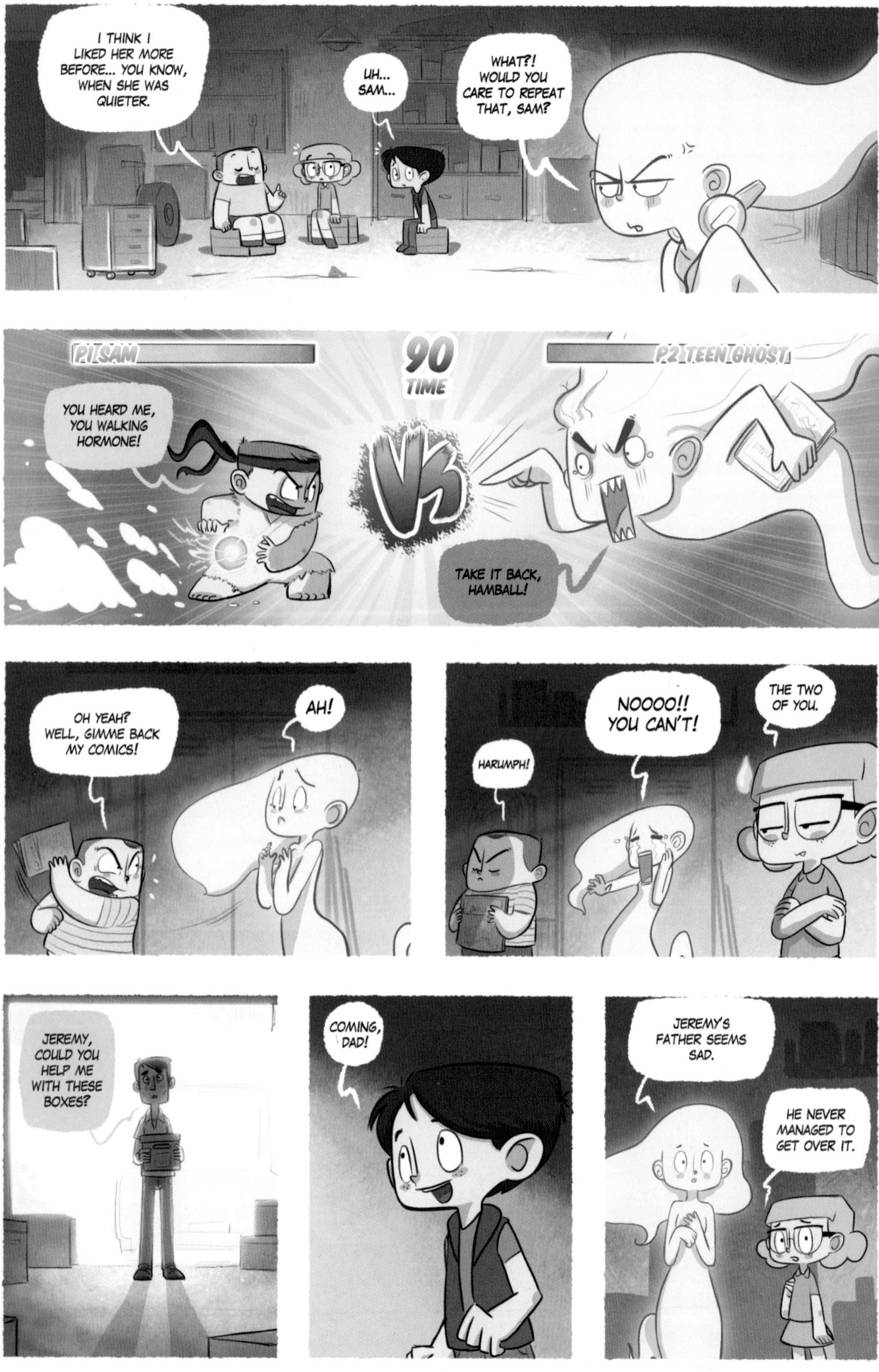
I THINK I LIKED HER MORE BEFORE... YOU KNOW, WHEN SHE WAS QUIETER.
UH... SAM...
WHAT?! WOULD YOU CARE TO REPEAT THAT, SAM?
P.1 SAM
90 TIME
P.2 TEEN GHOST
YOU HEARD ME, YOU WALKING HORMONE!
VS
TAKE IT BACK, HAMBALL!
OH YEAH? WELL, GIMME BACK MY COMICS!
AH!
HARUMPH!
NOOOO!! YOU CAN'T!
THE TWO OF YOU.
JEREMY, COULD YOU HELP ME WITH THESE BOXES?
COMING, DAD!
JEREMY'S FATHER SEEMS SAD.
HE NEVER MANAGED TO GET OVER IT.

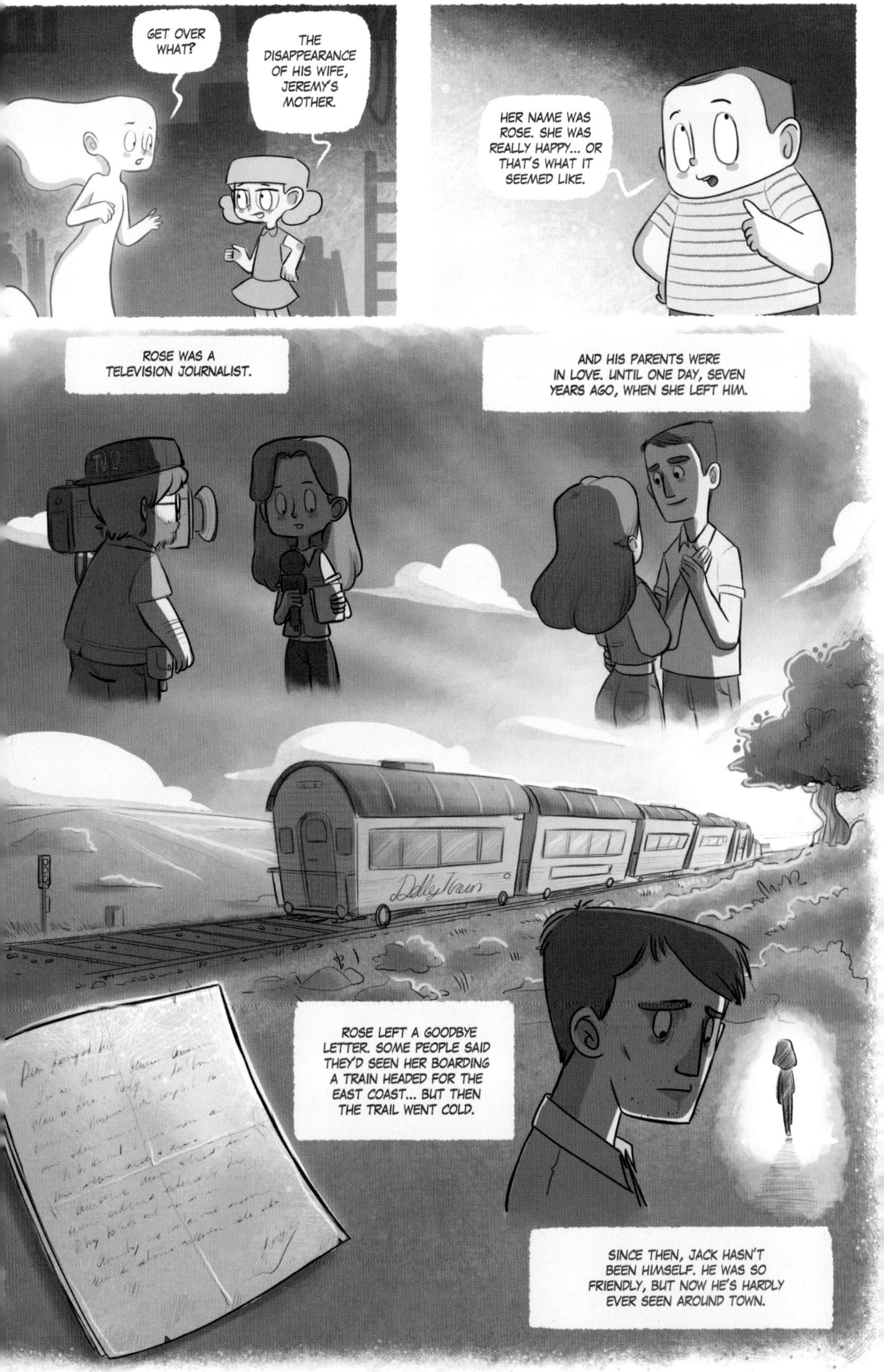
GET OVER WHAT?
THE DISAPPEARANCE OF HIS WIFE, JEREMY'S MOTHER.
HER NAME WAS ROSE. SHE WAS REALLY HAPPY... OR THAT'S WHAT IT SEEMED LIKE.
ROSE WAS A TELEVISION JOURNALIST.
AND HIS PARENTS WERE IN LOVE. UNTIL ONE DAY, SEVEN YEARS AGO, WHEN SHE LEFT HIM.
ROSE LEFT A GOODBYE LETTER. SOME PEOPLE SAID THEY'D SEEN HER BOARDING A TRAIN HEADED FOR THE EAST COAST... BUT THEN THE TRAIL WENT COLD.
SINCE THEN, JACK HASN'T BEEN HIMSELF. HE WAS SO FRIENDLY, BUT NOW HE'S HARDLY EVER SEEN AROUND TOWN.

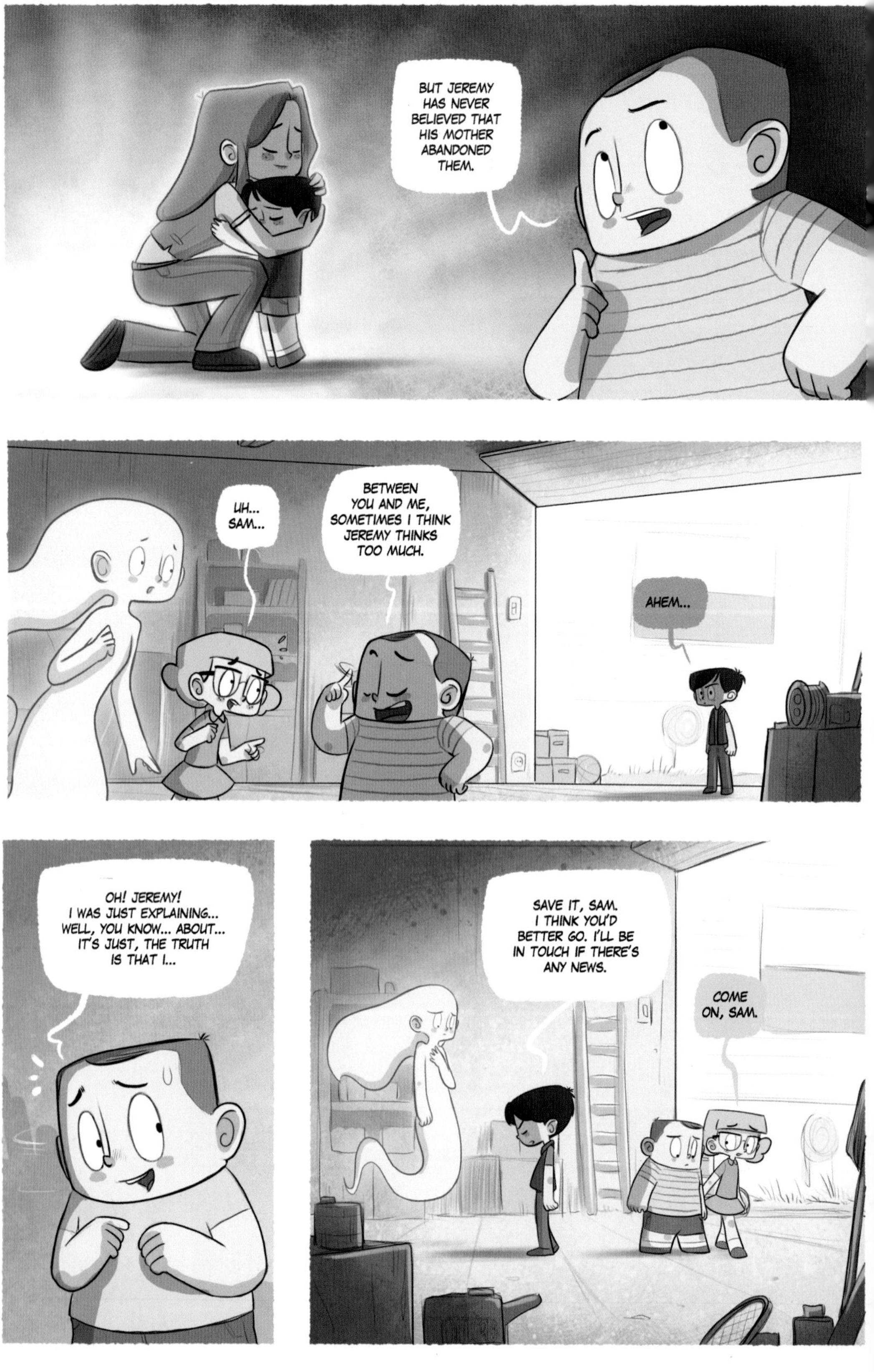
BUT JEREMY HAS NEVER BELIEVED THAT HIS MOTHER ABANDONED THEM.
UH... SAM...
BETWEEN YOU AND ME, SOMETIMES I THINK JEREMY THINKS TOO MUCH.
AHEM...
OH! JEREMY! I WAS JUST EXPLAINING... WELL, YOU KNOW... ABOUT... IT'S JUST, THE TRUTH IS THAT I...
SAVE IT, SAM. I THINK YOU'D BETTER GO. I'LL BE IN TOUCH IF THERE'S ANY NEWS.
COME ON, SAM.

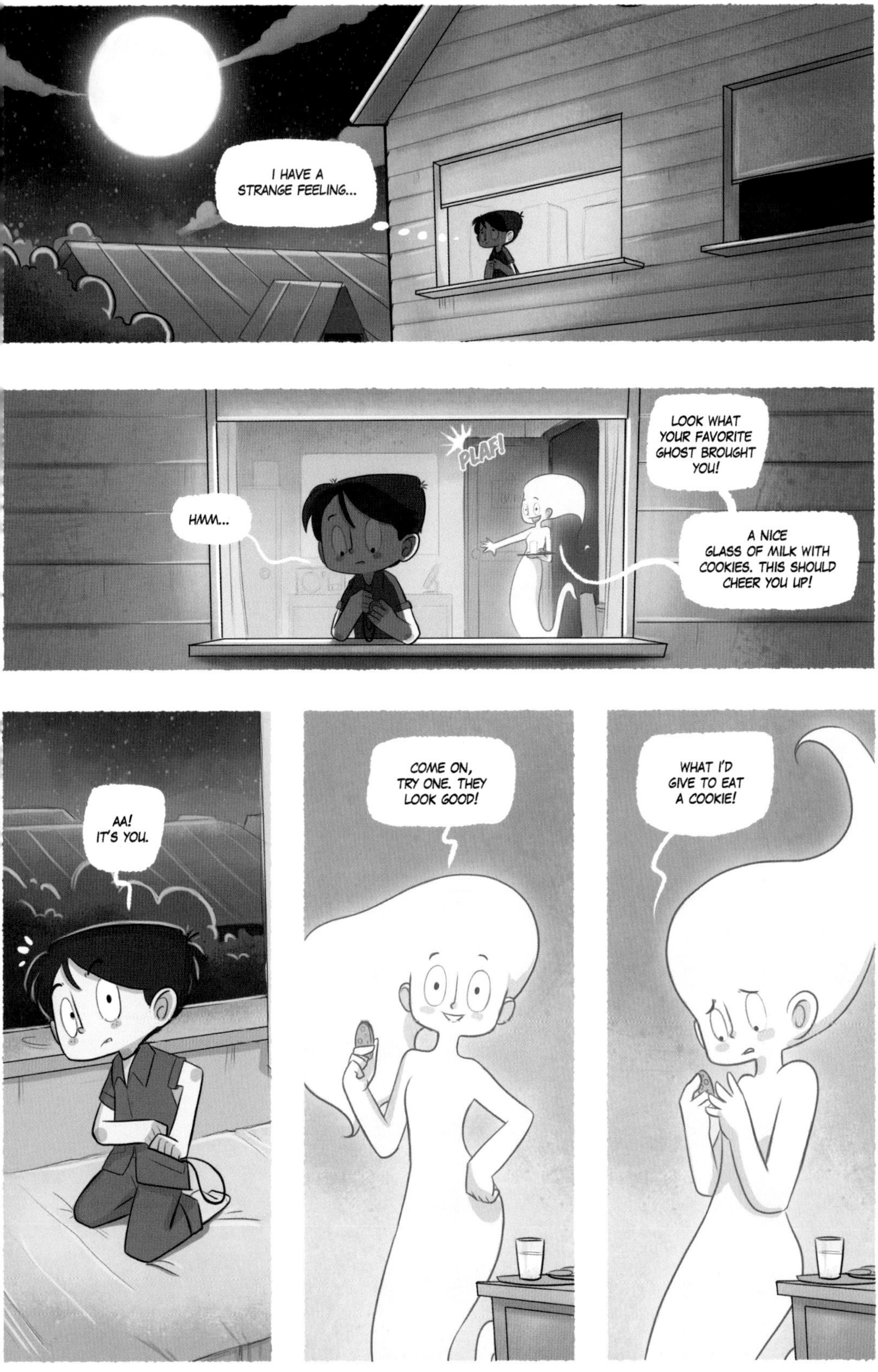
I HAVE A STRANGE FEELING...
PLAF!
HMM...
LOOK WHAT YOUR FAVORITE GHOST BROUGHT YOU!
A NICE GLASS OF MILK WITH COOKIES. THIS SHOULD CHEER YOU UP!
AA! IT'S YOU.
COME ON, TRY ONE. THEY LOOK GOOD!
WHAT I'D GIVE TO EAT A COOKIE!

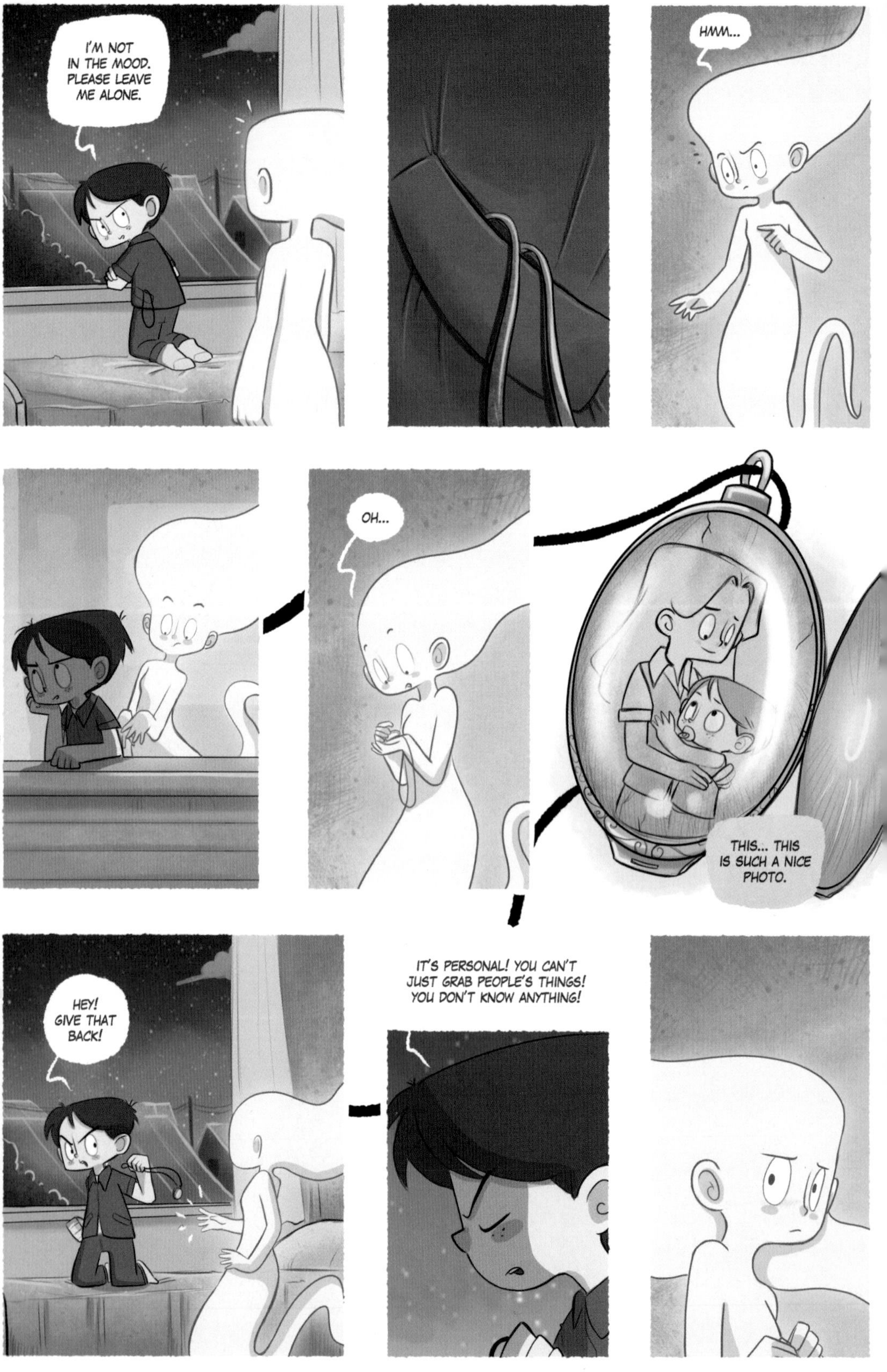
I'M NOT IN THE MOOD. PLEASE LEAVE ME ALONE.
HMM...
OH...
THIS... THIS IS SUCH A NICE PHOTO.
HEY! GIVE THAT BACK!
IT'S PERSONAL! YOU CAN'T JUST GRAB PEOPLE'S THINGS! YOU DON'T KNOW ANYTHING!

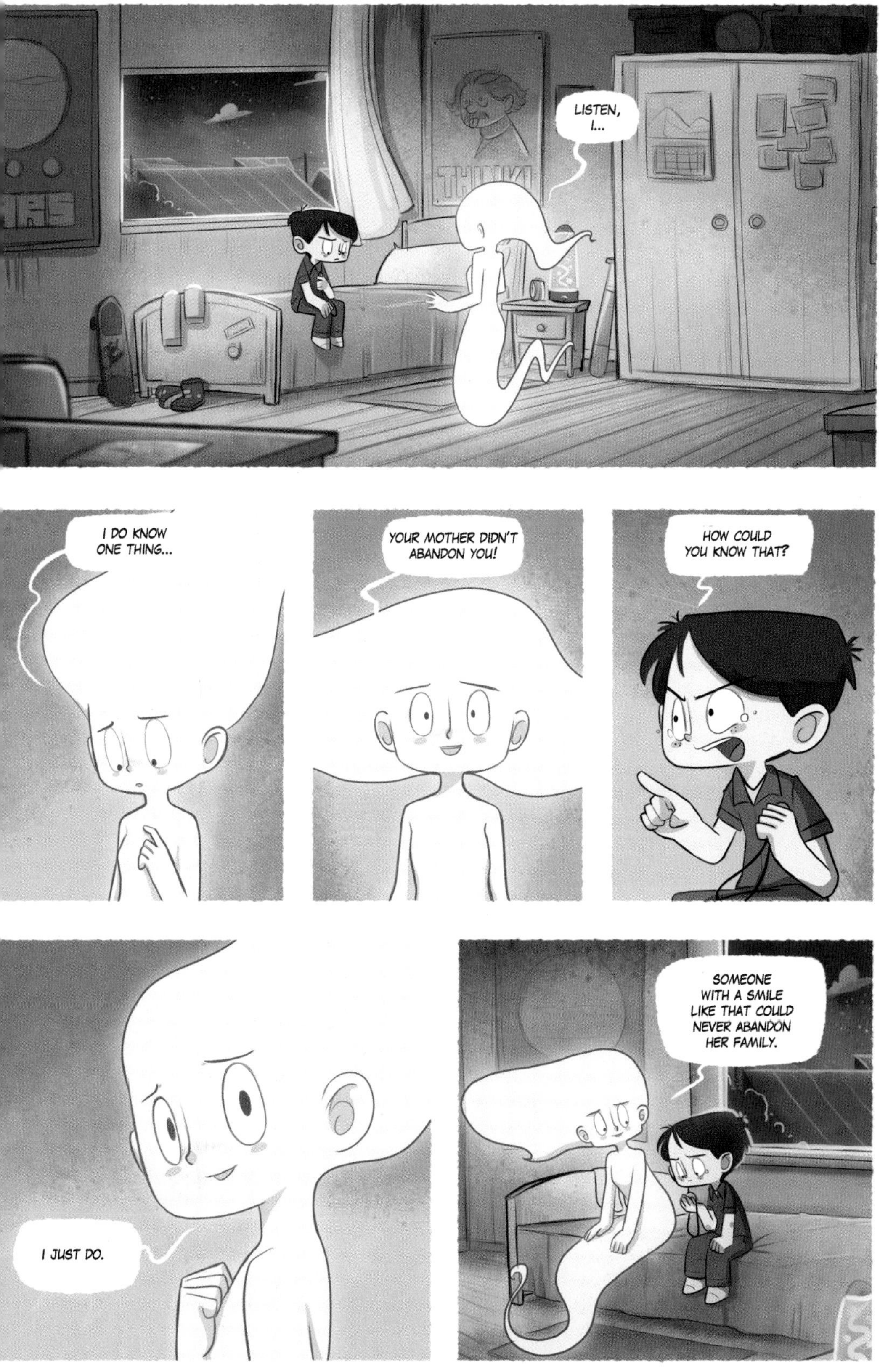
LISTEN, I...
I DO KNOW ONE THING...
YOUR MOTHER DIDN'T ABANDON YOU!
HOW COULD YOU KNOW THAT?
I JUST DO.
SOMEONE WITH A SMILE LIKE THAT COULD NEVER ABANDON HER FAMILY.

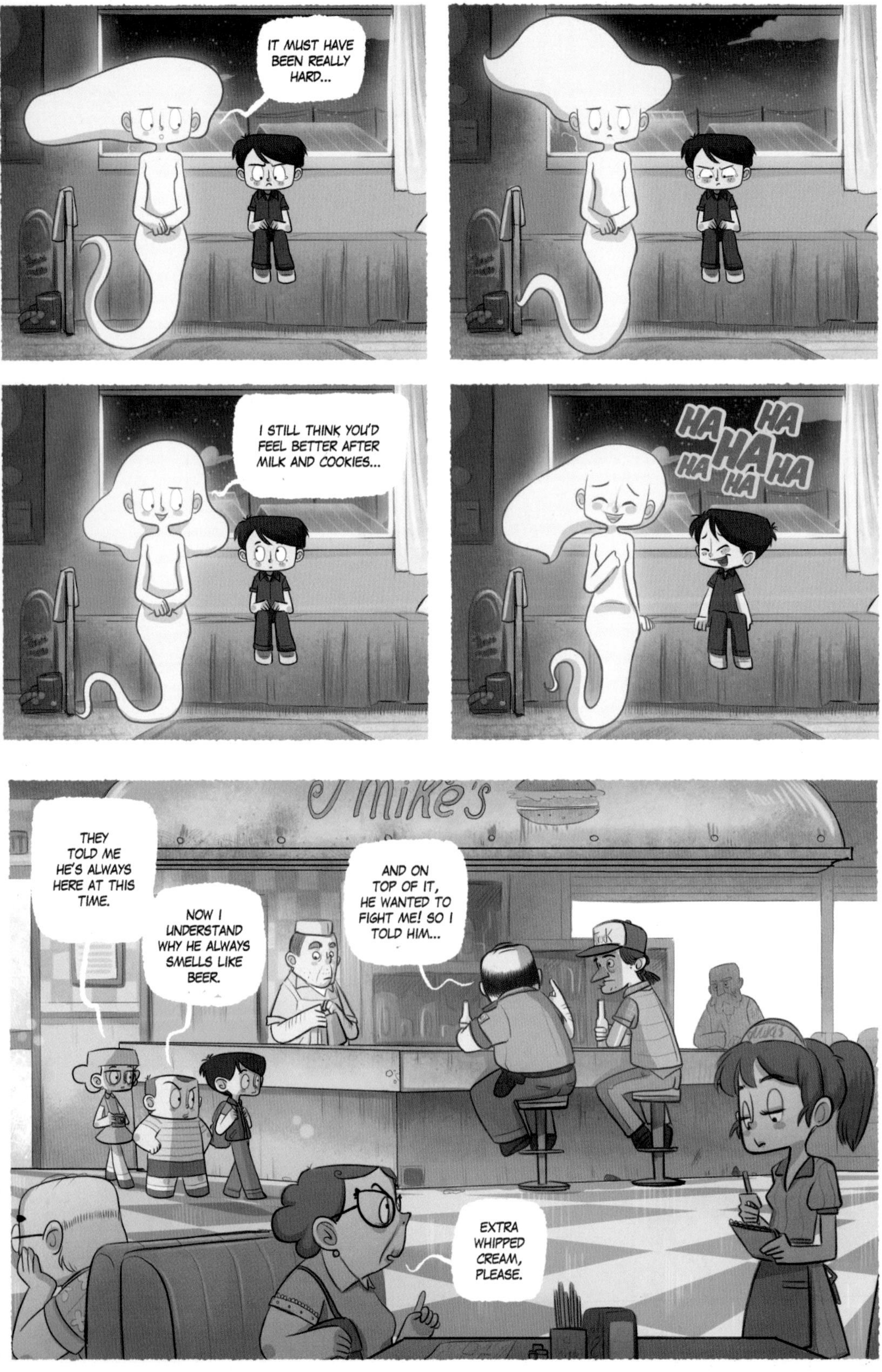
IT MUST HAVE BEEN REALLY HARD...
I STILL THINK YOU'D FEEL BETTER AFTER MILK AND COOKIES...
HA HA HA HA HA HA HA
Mike's
THEY TOLD ME HE'S ALWAYS HERE AT THIS TIME.
NOW I UNDERSTAND WHY HE ALWAYS SMELLS LIKE BEER.
AND ON TOP OF IT, HE WANTED TO FIGHT ME! SO I TOLD HIM...
EXTRA WHIPPED CREAM, PLEASE.

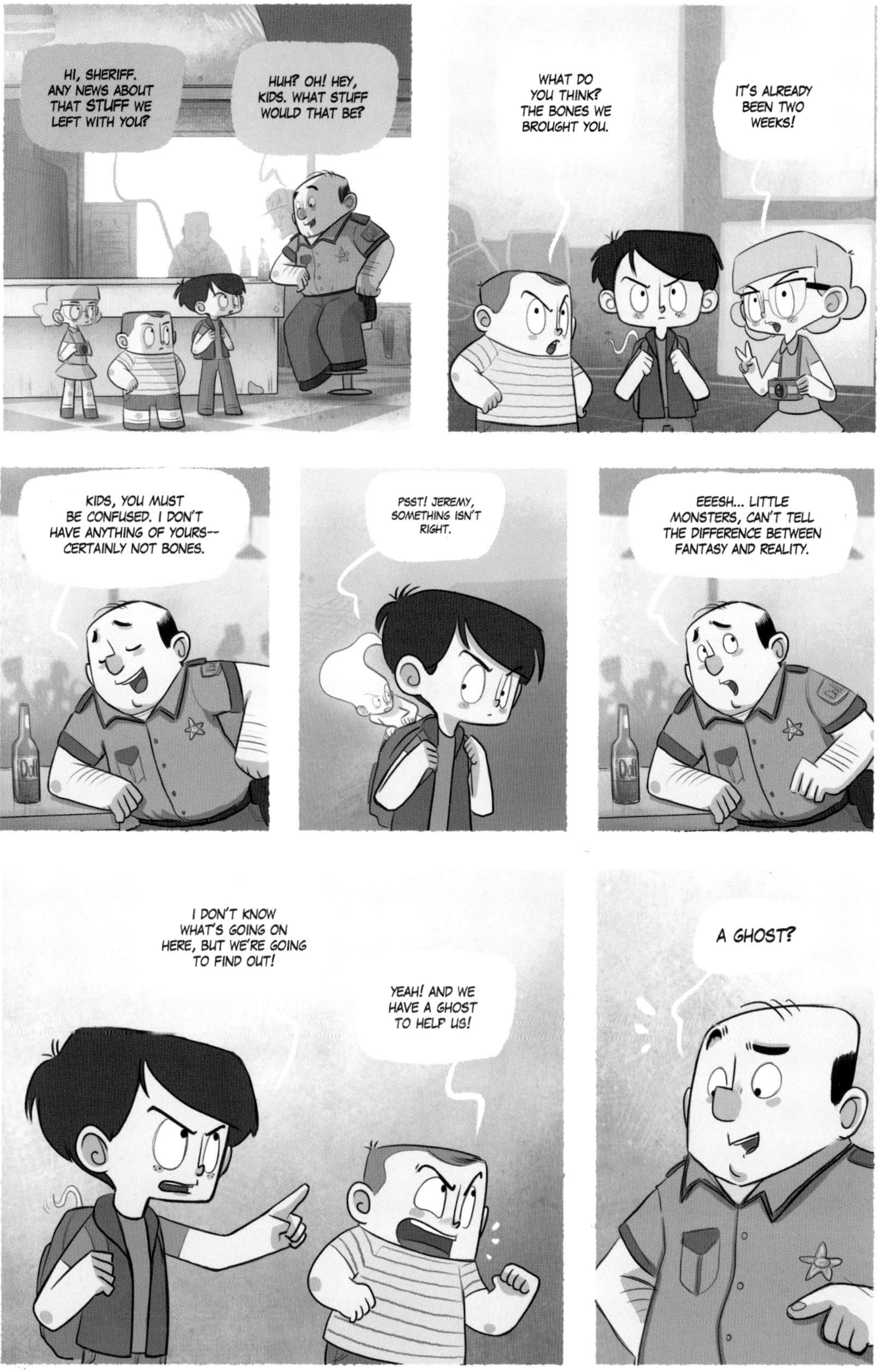
HI, SHERIFF. ANY NEWS ABOUT THAT STUFF WE LEFT WITH YOU?
HUH? OH! HEY, KIDS. WHAT STUFF WOULD THAT BE?
WHAT DO YOU THINK? THE BONES WE BROUGHT YOU.
IT'S ALREADY BEEN TWO WEEKS!
KIDS, YOU MUST BE CONFUSED. I DON'T HAVE ANYTHING OF YOURS-- CERTAINLY NOT BONES.
PSST! JEREMY, SOMETHING ISN'T RIGHT.
EEESH... LITTLE MONSTERS, CAN'T TELL THE DIFFERENCE BETWEEN FANTASY AND REALITY.
I DON'T KNOW WHAT'S GOING ON HERE, BUT WE'RE GOING TO FIND OUT!
YEAH! AND WE HAVE A GHOST TO HELP US!
A GHOST?

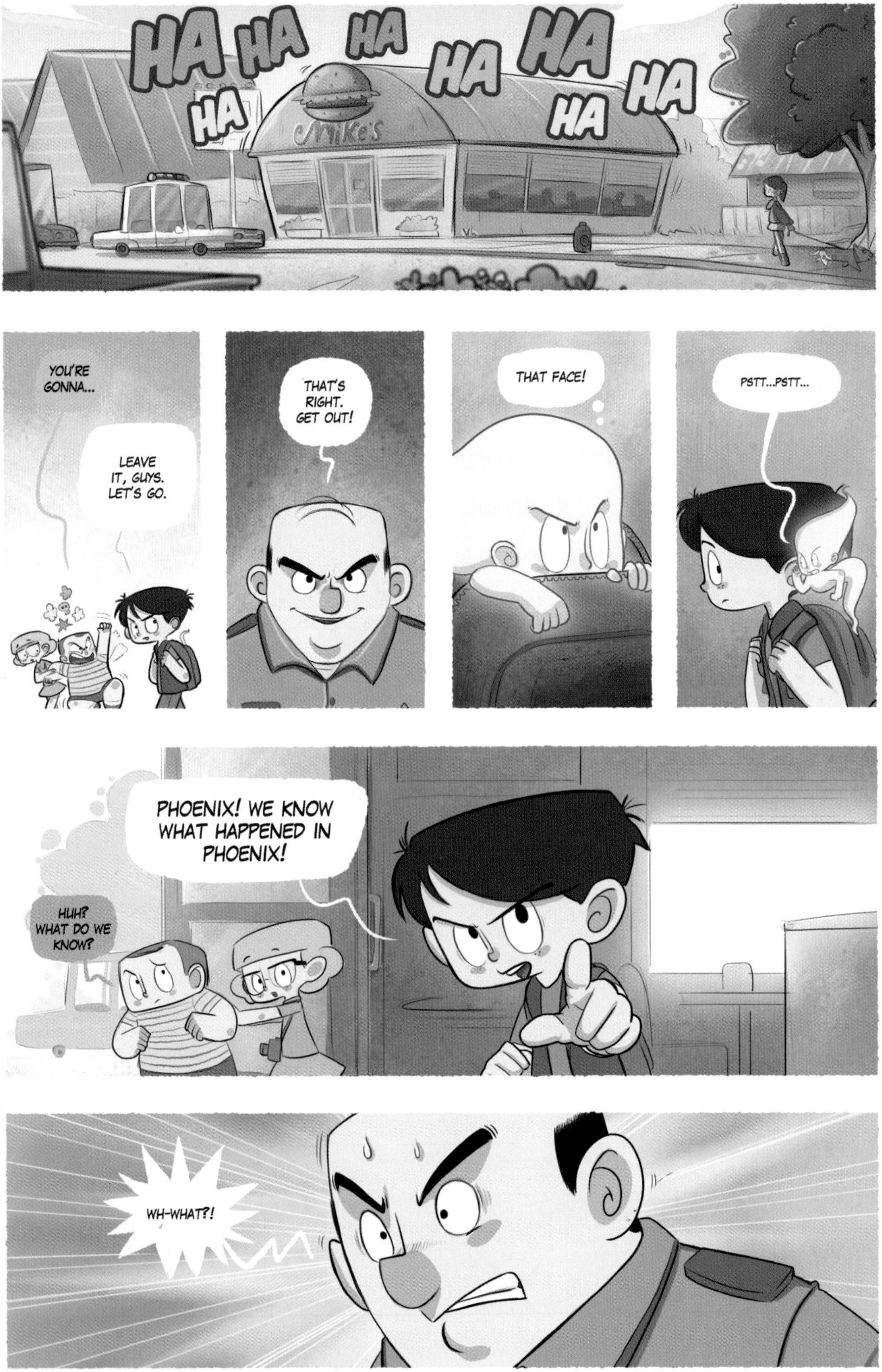

HA HA HA HA HA HA HA HA HA
YOU'RE GONNA...
LEAVE IT, GUYS. LET'S GO.
THAT'S RIGHT. GET OUT!
THAT FACE!
PSTT...PSTT...
PHOENIX! WE KNOW WHAT HAPPENED IN PHOENIX!
HUH? WHAT DO WE KNOW?
WH-WHAT?!

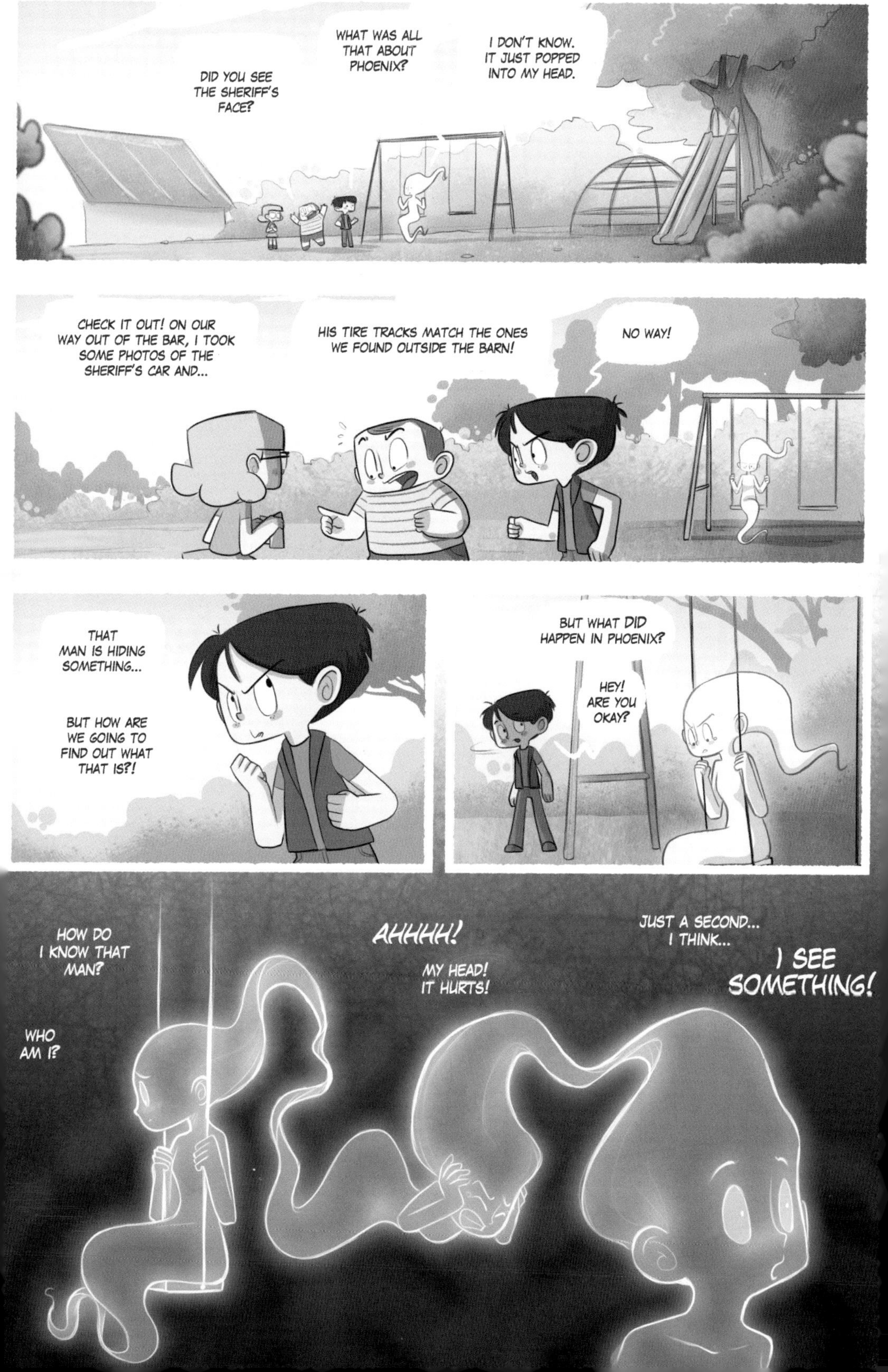
DID YOU SEE THE SHERIFF'S FACE?
WHAT WAS ALL THAT ABOUT PHOENIX?
I DON'T KNOW. IT JUST POPPED INTO MY HEAD.
CHECK IT OUT! ON OUR WAY OUT OF THE BAR, I TOOK SOME PHOTOS OF THE SHERIFF'S CAR AND...
HIS TIRE TRACKS MATCH THE ONES WE FOUND OUTSIDE THE BARN!
NO WAY!
THAT MAN IS HIDING SOMETHING...
BUT HOW ARE WE GOING TO FIND OUT WHAT THAT IS?!
BUT WHAT DID HAPPEN IN PHOENIX?
HEY! ARE YOU OKAY?
HOW DO I KNOW THAT MAN?
WHO AM I?
AHHHH!
MY HEAD! IT HURTS!
JUST A SECOND... I THINK...
I SEE SOMETHING!

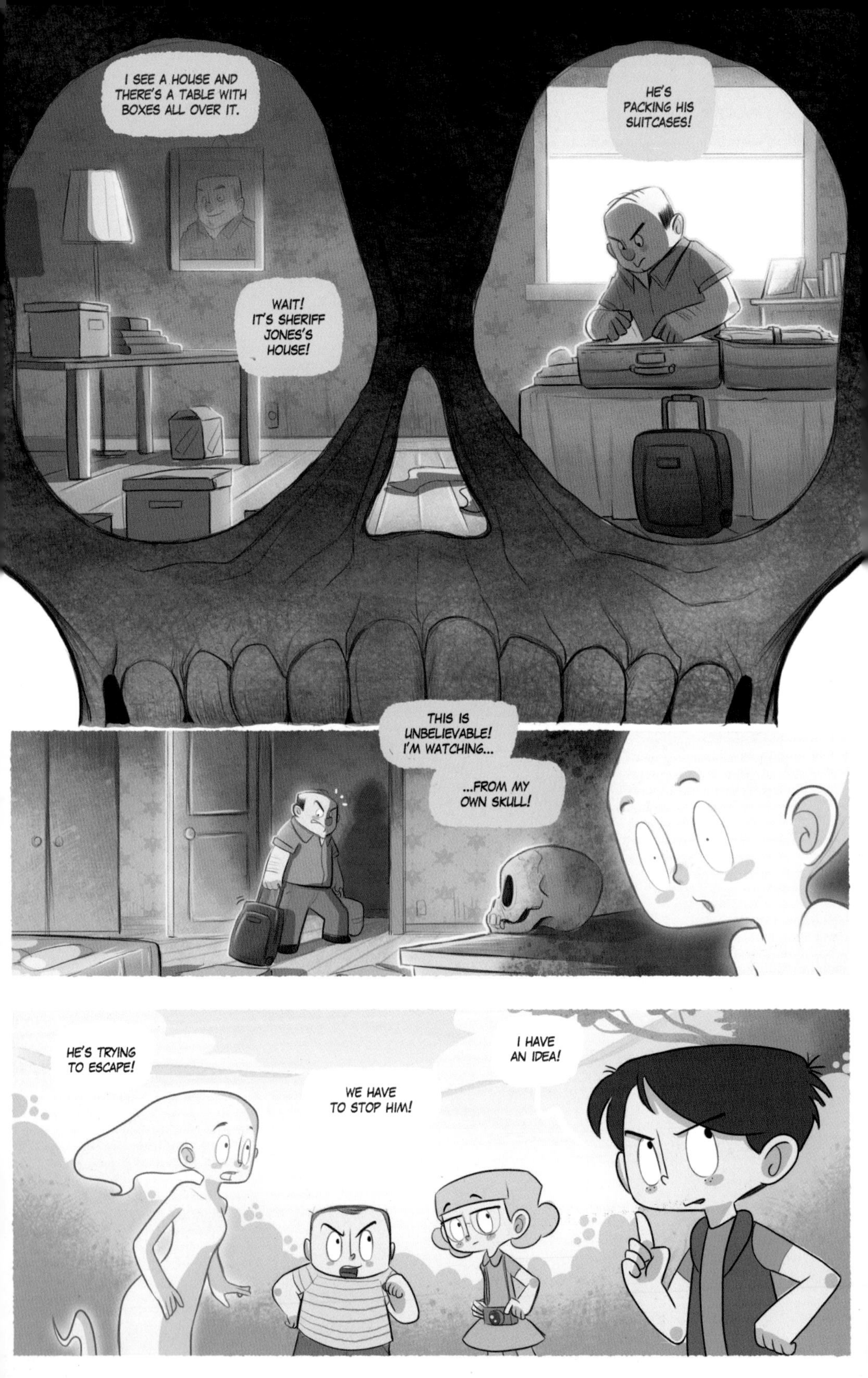
I SEE A HOUSE AND THERE'S A TABLE WITH BOXES ALL OVER IT.
WAIT! IT'S SHERIFF JONES'S HOUSE!
HE'S PACKING HIS SUITCASES!
THIS IS UNBELIEVABLE! I'M WATCHING...
...FROM MY OWN SKULL!
HE'S TRYING TO ESCAPE!
WE HAVE TO STOP HIM!
I HAVE AN IDEA!

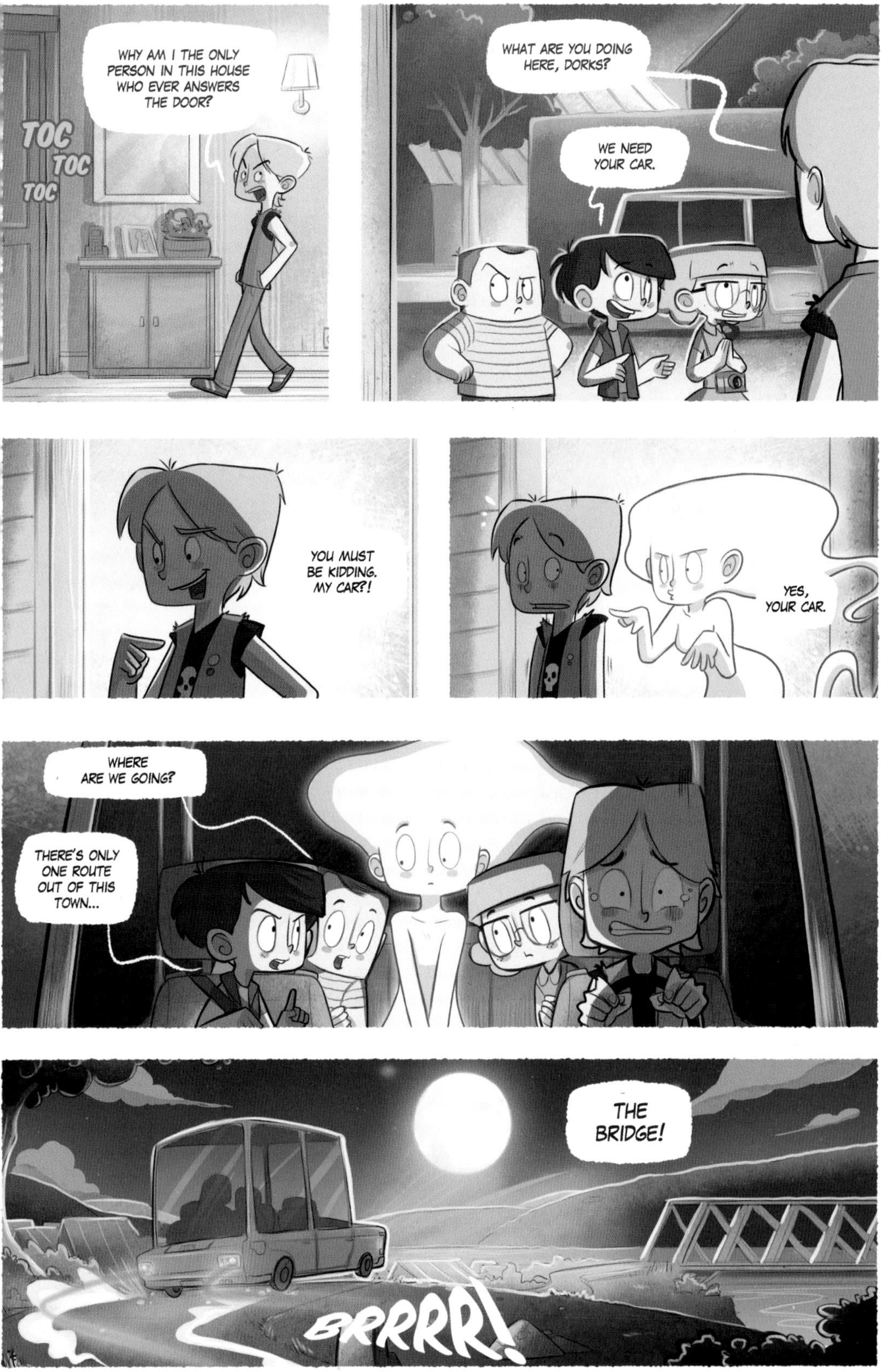
TOC
TOC
TOC
WHY AM I THE ONLY PERSON IN THIS HOUSE WHO EVER ANSWERS THE DOOR?
WHAT ARE YOU DOING HERE, DORKS?
WE NEED YOUR CAR.
YOU MUST BE KIDDING. MY CAR?!
YES, YOUR CAR.
WHERE ARE WE GOING?
THERE'S ONLY ONE ROUTE OUT OF THIS TOWN...
THE BRIDGE!
BRRRR!

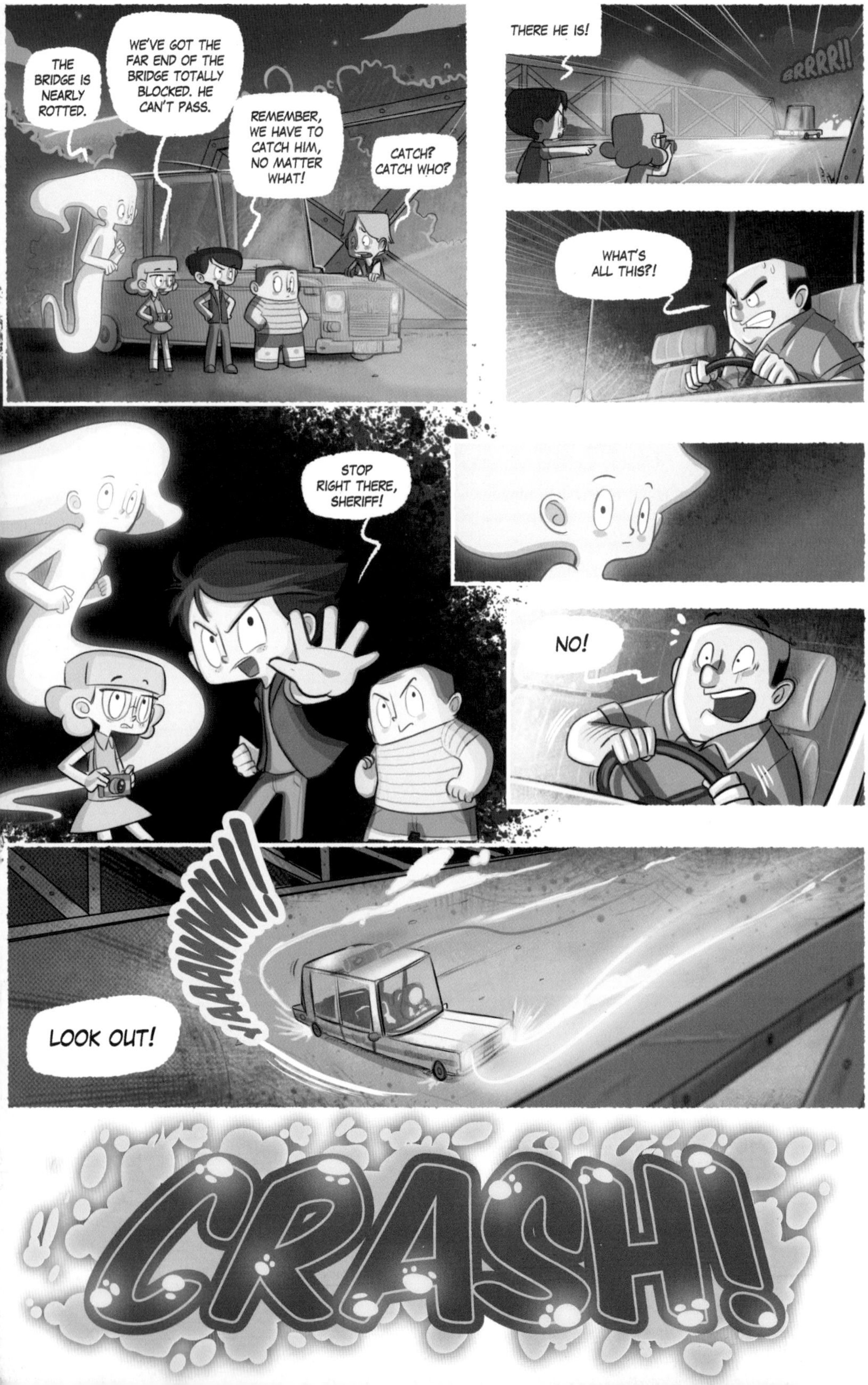
THE BRIDGE IS NEARLY ROTTED.
WE'VE GOT THE FAR END OF THE BRIDGE TOTALLY BLOCKED. HE CAN'T PASS.
REMEMBER, WE HAVE TO CATCH HIM, NO MATTER WHAT!
CATCH? CATCH WHO?
THERE HE IS!
BRRRR!!
WHAT'S ALL THIS?!
STOP RIGHT THERE, SHERIFF!
NO!
LOOK OUT!
AAAAWWW!
CRASH!

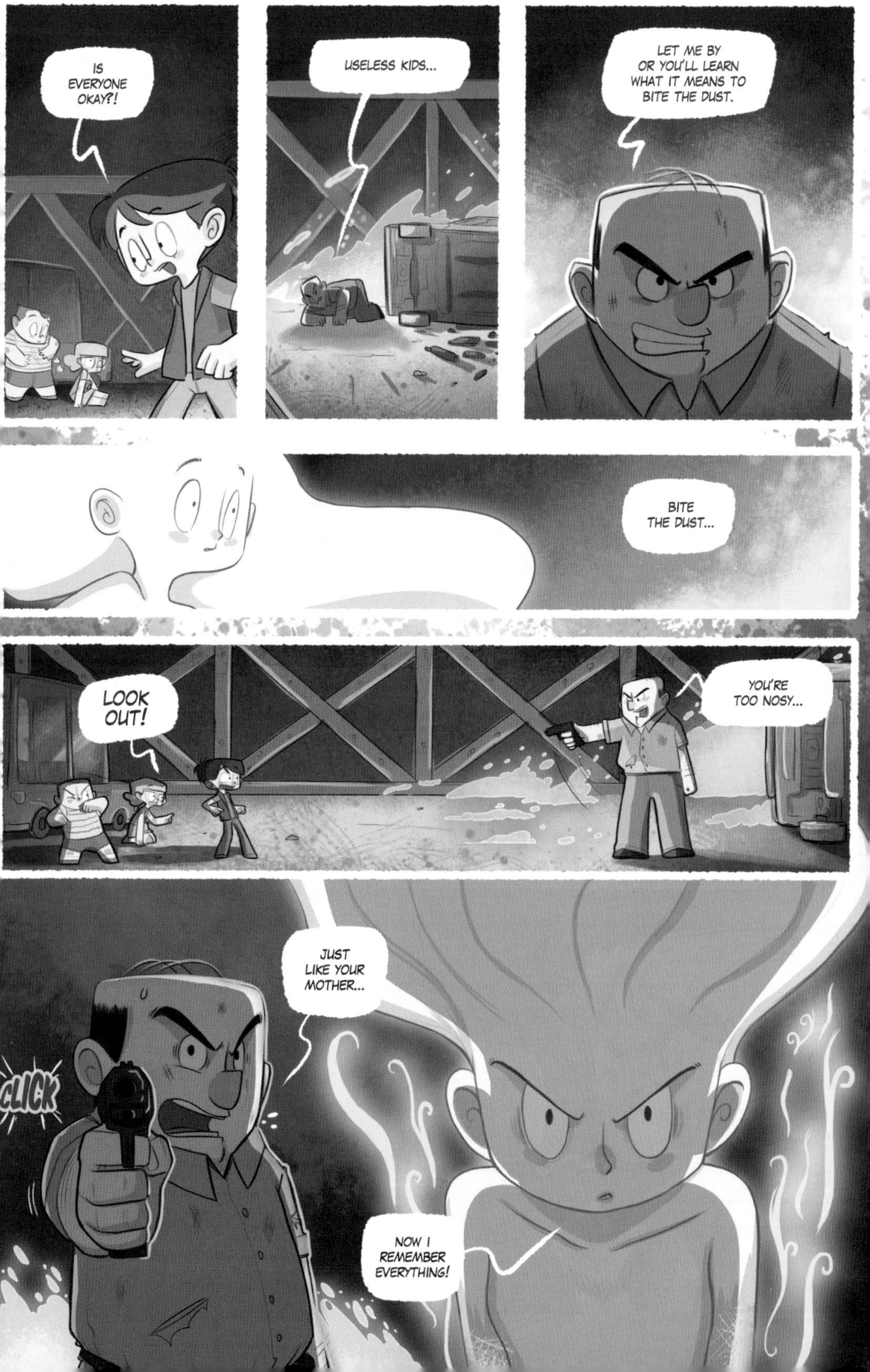
IS
EVERYONE
OKAY?!
USELESS KIDS...
LET ME BY
OR YOU'LL LEARN
WHAT IT MEANS TO
BITE THE DUST.
BITE
THE DUST...
LOOK
OUT!
YOU'RE
TOO NOSY...
JUST
LIKE YOUR
MOTHER...
CLICK
NOW I
REMEMBER
EVERYTHING!

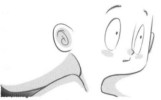

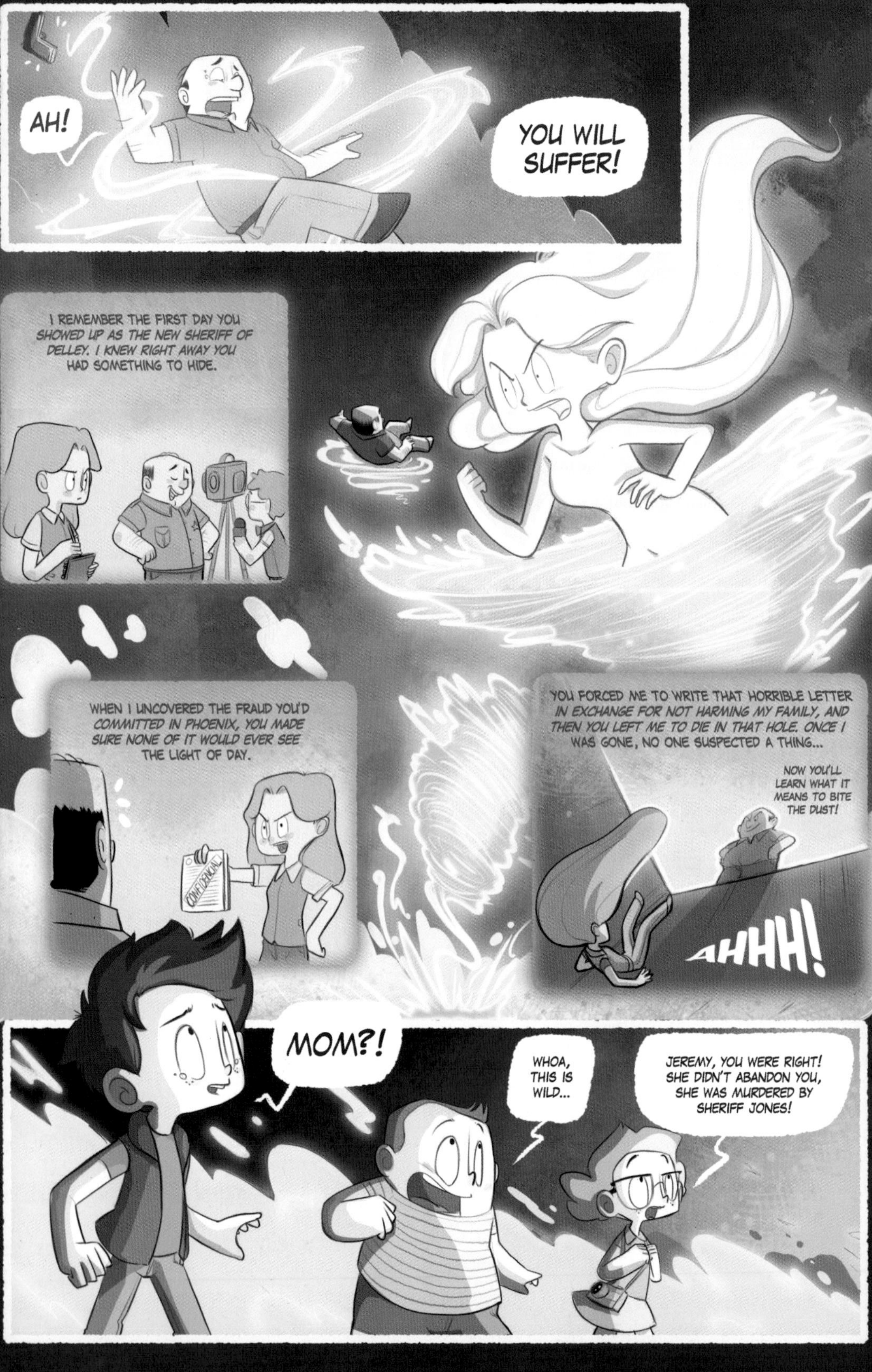
AH!
YOU WILL SUFFER!
I REMEMBER THE FIRST DAY YOU SHOWED UP AS THE NEW SHERIFF OF DELLEY. I KNEW RIGHT AWAY YOU HAD SOMETHING TO HIDE.
WHEN I UNCOVERED THE FRAUD YOU'D COMMITTED IN PHOENIX, YOU MADE SURE NONE OF IT WOULD EVER SEE THE LIGHT OF DAY.
CONFIDENTIAL
YOU FORCED ME TO WRITE THAT HORRIBLE LETTER IN EXCHANGE FOR NOT HARMING MY FAMILY, AND THEN YOU LEFT ME TO DIE IN THAT HOLE. ONCE I WAS GONE, NO ONE SUSPECTED A THING...
NOW YOU'LL LEARN WHAT IT MEANS TO BITE THE DUST!
AHHH!
MOM?!
WHOA, THIS IS WILD...
JEREMY, YOU WERE RIGHT! SHE DIDN'T ABANDON YOU, SHE WAS MURDERED BY SHERIFF JONES!

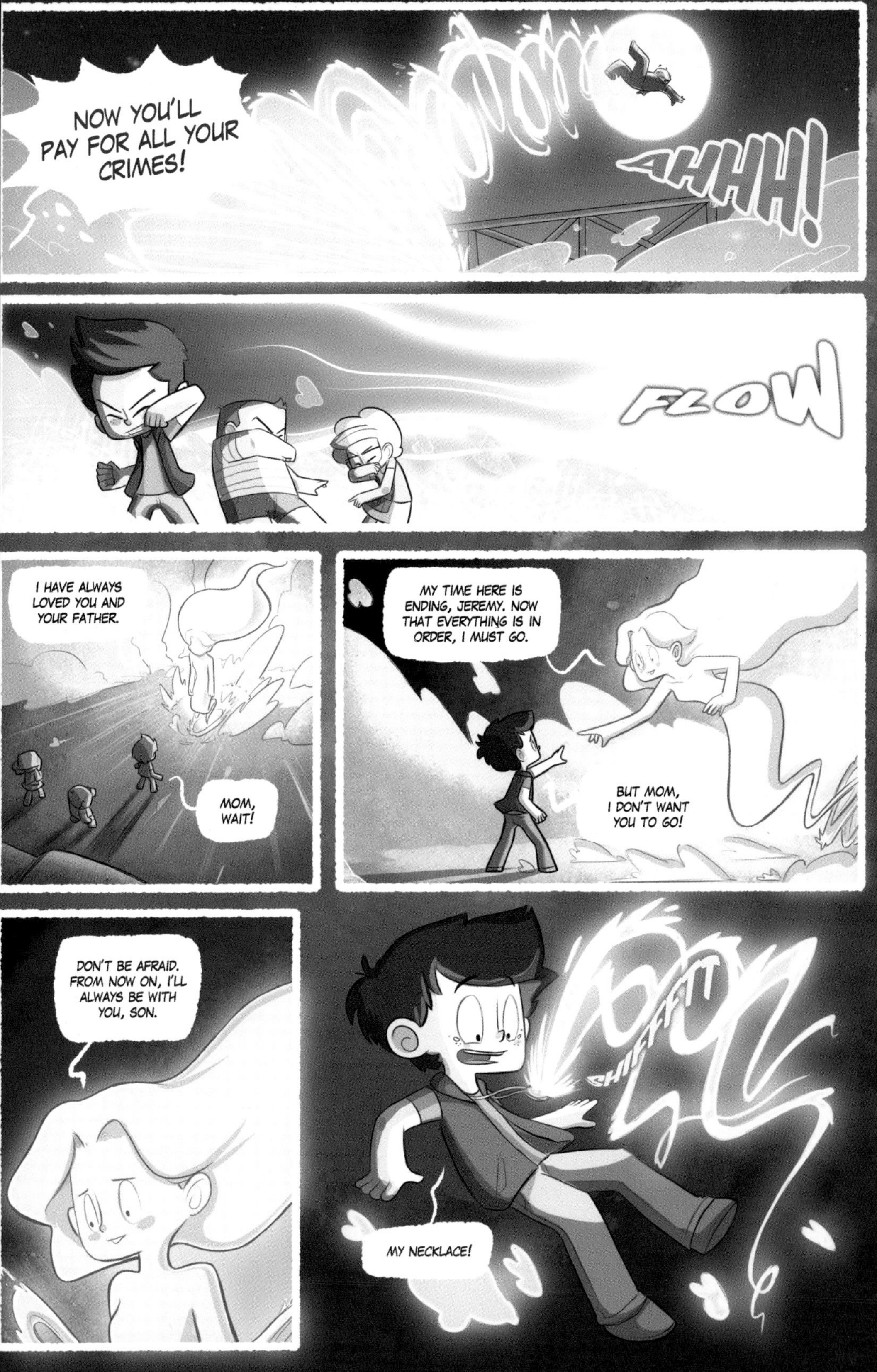
NOW YOU'LL PAY FOR ALL YOUR CRIMES!
AHHHH!
FLOW
I HAVE ALWAYS LOVED YOU AND YOUR FATHER.
MOM, WAIT!
MY TIME HERE IS ENDING, JEREMY. NOW THAT EVERYTHING IS IN ORDER, I MUST GO.
BUT MOM, I DON'T WANT YOU TO GO!
DON'T BE AFRAID. FROM NOW ON, I'LL ALWAYS BE WITH YOU, SON.
SHIFFFT!
MY NECKLACE!

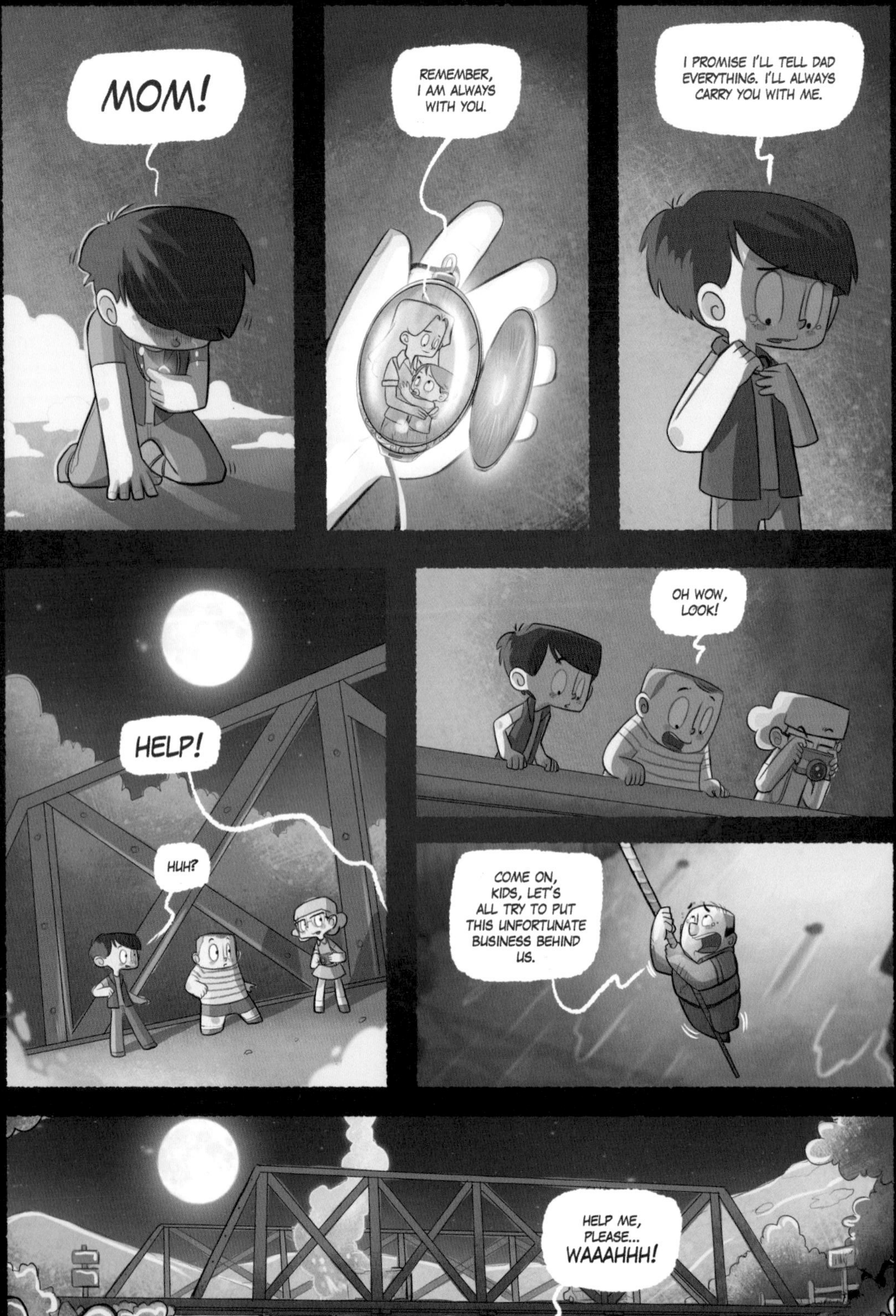
MOM!
REMEMBER, I AM ALWAYS WITH YOU.
I PROMISE I'LL TELL DAD EVERYTHING. I'LL ALWAYS CARRY YOU WITH ME.
HELP!
HUH?
OH WOW, LOOK!
COME ON, KIDS, LET'S ALL TRY TO PUT THIS UNFORTUNATE BUSINESS BEHIND US.
HELP ME, PLEASE... WAAAHHH!

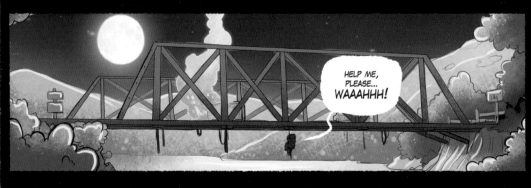

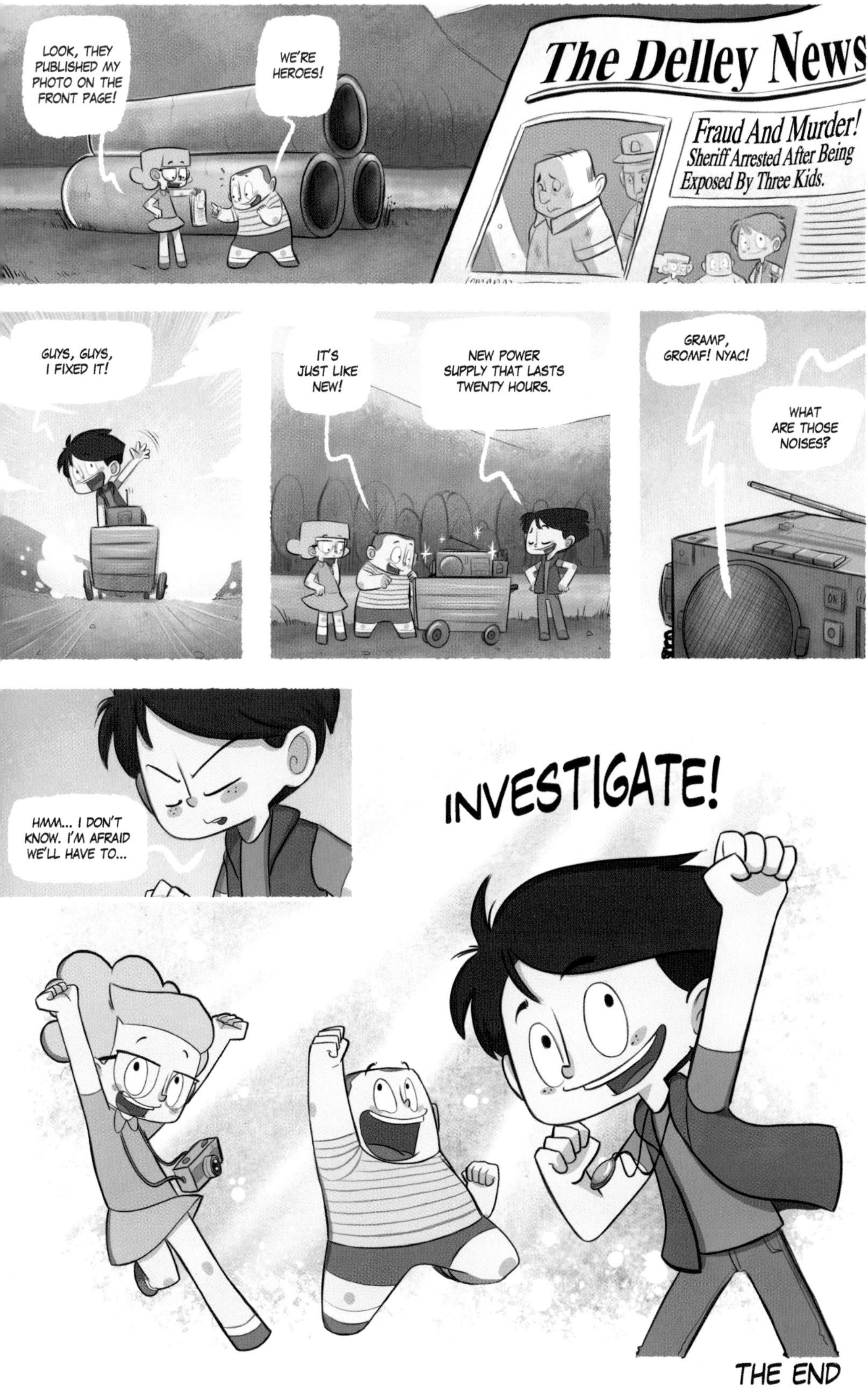
LOOK, THEY PUBLISHED MY PHOTO ON THE FRONT PAGE!
WE'RE HEROES!
The Delley News
Fraud And Murder!
Sheriff Arrested After Being Exposed By Three Kids.
GUYS, GUYS, I FIXED IT!
IT'S JUST LIKE NEW!
NEW POWER SUPPLY THAT LASTS TWENTY HOURS.
GRAMP, GROMF! NYAC!
WHAT ARE THOSE NOISES?
HMM... I DON'T KNOW. I'M AFRAID WE'LL HAVE TO...
INVESTIGATE!
THE END

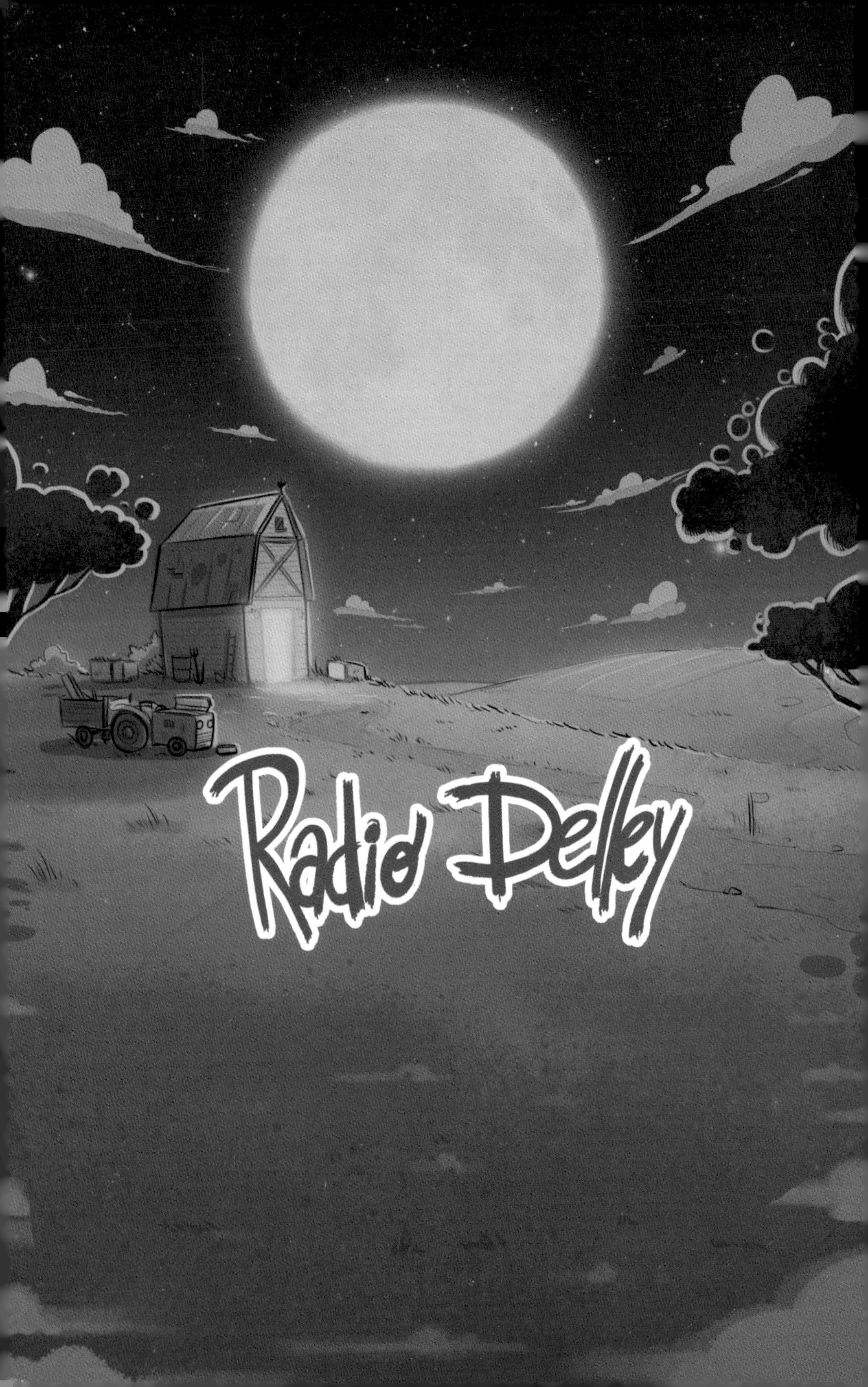
Radio Delley